TALES FROM
BUNNY WOOD

CONTENTS

This book is dedicated to Liz, for all her hard work behind
the scenes putting the finished stories and illustrations together.

To Elliott, who enjoyed countless walks and husky adventures
around Bunny Wood and the lake.

To Dudley, for being a patient photography assistant on
our daily nature rambles.

And to all the creatures of places like Bunny Wood, past,
present and, hopefully, future.

FOREWORD

Although the place names 'Bunny Wood' and 'Bunny Wood Lake' exist only in this author's imagination, the location and the wildlife around which these stories are based are, for now at least, very real.

I have fond memories as a child playing and having lots of adventures in places just like 'Bunny Wood'. It all seems quite long ago now, but, in nature's scheme of things, not that long at all.

Sadly, due mainly to the increased demands of a growing human population, such places are in decline.

Even as these stories were being written, houses and other brick and concrete developments are encroaching on the borders of Bunny Wood.

As each year passes, I see more and more human waste; bottles, tins, plastic food and snack bags, etc., thoughtlessly thrown onto pathways, into ditches and even in the lake itself.

The powers that be often seem to be on a mission to 'sanitize' the area; cutting down trees around the lake, clearing away brambles and other bushes, even reed beds which are perfect nesting places for waterfowl.

In addition a lot of time and, presumably, a lot of money, is regularly spent in cutting back dandelions and other wildflowers along the edges of walkways during spring and summer in an effort to keep the area 'tidy'.

Let's not forget two important factors about our dwindling, semi-suburban natural oases.

Firstly, I'm sure that what mostly brings people to visit, relax in and walk around such places is to see the wildlife; feeding the ducks, geese and swans, taking photographs of birds, rabbits and squirrels and so on.

Secondly, what brings such diverse wildlife, such as we have on 'Bunny Wood Lake' for example, are trees, reed beds and bushes to make homes in, as well as food to eat; brambles, berries and nuts from trees, wildflowers and grasses.

One of the more serious impacts on the environment for all of us is the decline of bees and other pollinators such as butterflies, moths and hoverflies. Without wildflowers and what we call 'weeds', the pollinators cannot feed and do their job.

I hope that whoever reads these stories will realise how important areas like this are to the well-being of us all, and will try to do whatever they can to help preserve our rich diversity of flora and fauna.

I, for one, don't want to see the day when the *real* 'Bunny Wood' exists only as a memory in the pages of this book.

INTRODUCTION

Bunny Wood is a peaceful place resting on the shores of a small lake. Its usual inhabitants are rabbits, squirrels, birds and all manner of waterfowl and wildlife, even the occasional cat. These are the creatures that we can see, during daylight hours at least. There are also fairies that we don't usually see, but evidence of their presence is all around if you know where to look.

On the far side of Bunny Wood Lake is Pigeon Wood, a dark, damp place, often peppered with bright red toadstools and mushroom villages. Pigeon Wood is mostly inhabited by pigeons and blackbirds, as many ground-dwelling creatures won't make their homes there, on account of it being a favoured hunting-ground for bogles. Only birds and the occasional squirrel find safety high up in the trees.

However, you don't have to venture far from the lake to encounter an even darker, less comforting world. A world of trees being slowly choked by a relentless army of ivy, carelessly discarded rubbish which bogles turn into ramshackle dwellings, and whose inhabitants are often much less welcoming than those of Bunny Wood.

Naturally, these places have many stories to tell.

We could begin these stories with 'Once upon a time...', but they happen *all* of the time for those who make time to linger.

Some of these stories you will find here.

MAP OF BUNNY WOOD AND LAKE

— 1 —

PIGNUTS AND DANDELION WINE

*T*o the casual passerby, Willow was like any other young rabbit in Bunny Wood, and you would be hard pushed to tell him apart from the others by all outward appearances, but there was something in his character that made him different from the rest.

Willow's story began early one beautiful late spring morning. One of those mornings when the sun warms your face from the moment you get up and go outside. Birds sang happily, ducks splish-splashed, enjoying their morning bath and all the woodland creatures busied themselves eating breakfast and looking forward to what the day might bring.

For Willow, food was something to be hurried, because there were other, more exciting things to be done, like playing with other spring-borns and exploring his still rather new world.

As was her habit while Willow was hurriedly munching on a breakfast of bitter-sweet dandelion leaves, his mother issued her daily warning, 'Don't wander too far' she said, 'and especially don't cross the path.

Remember, there are bogles on the other side, and they like nothing better than a rabbit stew for supper!'

The path which Willow's mother spoke of marked the boundary of Bunny Wood, beyond which were open fields and wasteland, dotted here and there with the occasional old dead tree.

The thing is, he was an adventurous little bunny this one, with a curious mind and a yearning to explore, and many a time since he had been allowed out on his own, Willow had stood at the edge of the path and wondered what was on the other side.

On this particular fine day, after playing for a while, Willow wandered off by himself, seeking an adventure. Today he was an intrepid explorer, carving his way through the undergrowth and looking into mysterious dark spaces between tree roots. After a while he came upon the path at the very edge of Bunny Wood. As usual, he looked out at the rather unwelcoming landscape in front of him. Only today he was feeling just a little more adventurous.

Not too far from where he sat was a big old tree stump with gnarly roots, covered in moss and ivy. 'I'll bet there are some interesting holes in that' he thought, 'perhaps even some unexplored tunnels!'

Willow remembered his mother's advice, which he usually heeded, but he then thought 'What if I just went and gandered about that tree? It's not too far, and there is still lots of daylight left.' He also felt sure that his mother once told him that bogles didn't like to come out in the daytime.

Well, of course, it didn't take much more than that to convince himself that it wouldn't really hurt to disobey his mother, just this once.

'Right!' he thought, 'That's it then. I'm off exploring!'

With that, Willow hopped across the path and through the patchy dry grass on the other side. Here and there were clusters of mushrooms and toadstools growing on decaying logs. Willow knew to keep clear of these because, as his mother had told him many times, some of them could give him a bad tummy ache. There were also clumps of wild flowers and plants, some of which he recognised from around his home, clinging together in small clearings. There were other bits and pieces he didn't recognise; sharp bits of shiny stuff which he carefully hopped around, so as not to cut his paws, and things that didn't smell very nice, rather like old cabbages.

Willow wrinkled his nose and began to think that perhaps this hadn't been such a good idea after all, but he was determined to at least take a look at the big old tree stump, which was quite close now.

As he pushed further on, he began to get a whiff of something else. He didn't know what it was, but it seemed to be coming from the tree stump and it smelled nice, making his tummy give out a hungry growl.

As he drew ever nearer, Willow found himself following a kind of path where the grass on either side was greener and lusher. Here there were more wildflowers and plants than before. It almost looked like a little garden.

He now saw that the tree was hollow, like a cave, and just inside the entrance was a big old pot sitting on top of a log fire. Willow sat for a moment, transfixed, his nose twitching, then a strange voice croaked, 'My, my! What's we got 'ere then? Why, it's a little bunnykin, if I'm not mistaken.' A wrinkled old face appeared from the dark interior of the hollowed-out tree, 'We don't tend to see many bunnykins round 'ere these days.'

Willow froze, as rabbits tend to do in uneasy situations, and found himself staring into the face of an old woman, a very old woman indeed, with long, straggly grey hair. He plucked up his courage, remembered his manners and said, 'I'm very sorry, but I over-hopped the path back there and my nose fair pulled me here it did, on account of that lovely smell.'

The old woman cackled, 'So, you likes the smell of my cooking, does you little bunnykin?'

Willow took a step backwards. He had almost forgotten where he was. 'Is you a bogle?' he asked nervously, 'My mother went and told me about bogles, she did. She said as how you catch bunnies and make rabbit stoup!'

The old bogle woman smiled and leaned forward. 'I think you means rabbit *stew*,' she said softly, 'There's no need to be afraid now. I have never eaten no bunnykins, and I never wants to neither.'

Despite her rather raggedy appearance, there was gentleness in the old woman's eyes that made Willow feel relaxed, even welcome. His nose twitched again, 'That's a lovely smell coming from your house,' he said, 'I wonder what it could be?'

The old woman smiled. 'You must forgive my manners little one' she said, 'It's been a long time since I's had any visitors.' She beckoned to him, 'Please, do come in,' she said, holding out a small round object, 'I'm stewin' pignuts for lunch, would you like some?'

Willow didn't know what pignuts were, but the aroma was just too good to resist. Despite the many warnings he'd had from his mother about bogles, there was something about this old woman that made him feel safe. A couple of hops later and he was inside the hollowed out tree.

It was quite dark inside, but there was enough light from the fire under the cooking pot for him to be able to look around. The house looked very cosy. There was a small table, a rickety-looking three-legged stool and, further back, a pile of straw, flattened down in the middle, which he reckoned to be the old woman's bed. Around the walls were shelves, lots of shelves, each one pile high with bottles, jars and boxes.

'Make yourself at home little bunnykin,' said the old woman, pointing to the table. 'Lunch is just about ready.'

Without a second thought, Willow hopped up onto the stool, and the old woman brought over a dish of the stew. 'Go on,' she said, 'tuck in before it gets cold.'

Well, let me tell you, Willow might have had no idea what a pignut was, but the stew was certainly one of the most delicious things he had ever tasted. He lapped away greedily, occasionally finding something soft and round, with a distinctly nutty taste. 'Is these pignuts?' he asked.

'Yes, my lovely,' said the old woman. 'Ave you never eaten one before?'

'No,' said Willow, trying to talk with his mouth full. 'It's scrummy! Where do they come from?'

The old woman smiled. 'They comes from under the ground my dear,' she said, 'at the very bottom of a pignut plant.'

'What's a pignut plant look like?' asked Willow.

'Well finish your stew,' replied the old woman, 'and I'll show you.'

Willow lapped up his stew in no time at all, even managing some seconds while the old bogle woman ate hers. Then, satisfied that he had eaten enough, she took him outside to her little 'garden', where she showed him what a pignut plant looked like.

'Ooh, ooh!' said Willow, excitedly, 'I've seen these around where I live.'

The old woman showed Willow how to carefully dig around the base of the plant and lift it to reveal the small brown 'nut' at the bottom of the stem.

'Well now you knows how to dig them up. They're nearly as tasty straight from the ground, as long as you cleans 'em,' she said. She was beginning to be quite taken with this charming little rabbit. 'I'll wager you like dandelions too.'

'Ooh,' said Willow, 'danderlines is one of my favourites.'

'Come back inside, and I'll show you some more tasty treats.'

They went inside, and the old woman took down some of the jars and bottles from her shelves.

'Now this one,' she said, opening a jar, 'is dandelion jam. Here, have a taste.'

Willow dipped his paw into the jar and licked off the dandelion jam. It was deliciously sweet.

'Now try this one.' The old woman opened a bottle and poured some liquid into his dish. Willow licked at it cautiously at first, then his eyes lit up and he lapped it all up in one go.

'Mm,' said Willow, 'that is the bestest-tasty water ever.'

'Nettle tea, my dear,' said the old woman. 'Very good for your tummy. I have all sorts like this on these 'ere shelves. Dandelion jam, all manner of berry conserves and teas, acorn flour, which makes the tastiest bread, let me tell you, pickled pignuts and dandelion wine. Mind you,' she said, 'that one's just for grown-ups!'

The old bogle woman seated herself on the stool and beckoned Willow to sit beside her, offering him a slice of acorn bread topped with sweet elderberry conserve, which he heartily accepted. 'You see, my lovely, when Mother Nature is your garden you will never go hungry.'

'Who's Mother Nature?' asked Willow, licking delicious elderberry from his lips. 'Does she live around here?'

The old woman smiled. 'She lives everywhere, my dear. Mother Nature is in the trees, the flowers, the water and, yes, in all little woodland creatures like you. And, if you let her, she'll look after you.'

'But I already have a mother,' said Willow, 'and *she* looks after me,'

'Of course she does,' said the old woman. 'But Mother Nature is your mother too. She is your mother's mother, and mine, and everyone else's.' She sighed and put her hands on her lap. 'I'm sorry to say though, little bunnykin, that many of my kind who once loved Mother Nature, respected her and gave thanks for all she provided, are of the opinion that they are better than her, and that they can take care of themselves without her help.'

'That's very sad,' said Willow.

'You just have to look around you,' said the old woman. 'All of this used to be a meadow, with all manner of wildflowers, bees and butterflies. Now most of the trees and plants round 'ere are gone; and they goes and leaves rubbish behind them everywhere. Mother Nature is struggling to cope with it all. With everything else she has to do, she ain't got time for cleaning up after them that don't respect her.'

Willow noticed a tear in the old woman's eye. 'One day soon,' she said, looking around her cosy little house, 'even this will be gone.'

'But why?' asked Willow.

'I'm afraid that many bogles is just too greedy and selfish,' said the old woman. 'They have forgotten the old ways of living off the land. They have become lazy and cruel. Why should they waste time growing food when they can just catch it, or steal it?'

'And they eat rabbit stoup,' said Willow.

'Yes my dear, I'm sorry to say.'

'I wish they was all like you,' said Willow. 'Can I come and visit you again?'

'I think perhaps it's best not to,' said the old woman. 'Your mother is right. It's becoming too dangerous for little creatures like you out here. Better that you stay in your own wood, where you'll be safer.'

'But what will happen to you?' asked Willow.

'Don't you go fretting about an old bogle like me,' said the old woman. 'If Mother Nature wants it, she'll find me another house and garden somewhere when the time comes.' She wiped her eye and stood up. 'Anyway, I reckon it's about time for you to be hopping along back home. You really don't want to be out here too long. Your mother will be worrying, and you must respect her, remember?'

'I will, I promise,' said Willow.

The old woman took a jar of dandelion jam from the shelf and handed it to Willow. 'Take this with you and share it with your loved ones.'

Willow took the jar and said farewell to the old woman. When he reached the path, he looked back towards her house, from where she gave him a little wave before going back inside.

When Willow got back home, he gave his mother the jar of dandelion jam and told her all about his lunch with the old woman. Needless to say, she was angry with him at first for crossing the path and going into a bogle's house. Afterwards though she forgave him, for even *she* knew that not all bogles were bad.

Some days later, out of curiosity, Willow made his way to the path again, just to look out at the bogle woman's house. When he got there the tree was gone. The grass had been cut to a stubble and there wasn't a flower to be seen anywhere; all that remained were piles of rubbish. Willow thought about the old woman, and was sad to think what might have happened to her, and what was happening so close to Bunny Wood. He could only hope that Mother Nature had found the old woman a new home. With a heavy heart, Willow turned and made his way back home.

It was now summertime in Bunny Wood, and the spring-borns were growing up fast. Willow was maturing into a fine, strong rabbit. He had learned to respect not only Mother Nature but his own mother too. Often, instead of playing, he would be out foraging for brambles, dandelions and of course pignuts, which were now his favourite treat.

Most days, his encounter with the old bogle woman would be in Willow's thoughts, and he would find himself pausing whilst nibbling on a dandelion leaf to wonder what had become of her.

There was talk among the creatures of Bunny Wood that bogles had settled on the wasteland beyond the path, and regular squirrel patrols had been established to warn of any attempt to cross the path into Bunny Wood. These were hard times indeed for any creature that depended on the fruits of Mother Nature; but for now at least, Bunny Wood was still a safe and bountiful place for a young rabbit to grow up in.

One fine summer morning Willow got up early, as he always did now, eager to be first out for breakfast. When he emerged into the sunlight he was caught by surprise.

A huge smile lit his face. For there, carefully placed at the entrance to the warren were three objects that he recognised at once; a jar of dandelion jam, a fair-sized pot of pignut stew – still warm – and a bottle of dandelion wine.

—— 2 ——

A HARD NUT TO CRACK

*A*utumn is a busy time of year for the inhabitants of Bunny Wood, especially for squirrels. On this particular fine autumn day, the sun was shining and all the trees were flaunting their golden finery. Bramble was busy, squirreling away up in the branches of an oak tree, scrumping and scrimping for his winter stores, when he spied something out of the corner of his eye; a large object hanging off a stout branch just below him.

As Bramble climbed down to get a closer look, his jaw dropped in amazement, for hanging right there in front of him was the biggest acorn he had ever seen.

'Oh my!' he thought. 'Now that is indeed a very tibble feast!'

Bramble reached down to test the weight of the acorn with his front paws.

'Mmm,' he thought. 'This is a heavy one. Perhaps I'll just crackle it here and get the meat out.' With that, he positioned himself so that he was hanging upside down on the branch by his back paws, and began gnawing at the acorn shell with his sharp teeth.

After what seemed like ages, Bramble was getting nowhere. In fact, there wasn't even a scratch on the humungous acorn, let alone a crackle.

A blackbird watching all of this, ever so slightly bemused, from a nearby post asked, 'What are you doing there, my dear squirrel?'

Bramble looked at the blackbird, frowning. 'I'm trying to crackle this nut so's I can eat it,' he said. 'But it's so hard I can't even get my teeth into it!'

'Why don't you try dropping it onto that old tree stump below?' the blackbird suggested. 'If that doesn't crackle it I don't know what will!'

'Mmm, that's not a half bad idea!' said Bramble. 'In fact it's more than half. Thank you Mr Blackbird.'

'My pleasure,' said the blackbird somewhat smugly. Then off he went in search of some juicy berries.

Bramble lowered himself again and began to nibble on the thicker than usual acorn stalk until, bit by bit, it came free and dropped down onto the hard tree stump below with a mighty WHOP! But instead of crackling, the nut merely bounced off and landed with a bit of a thump on a patch of damp moss. 'Humph!' he thought, 'Perhaps that was *less* than half an idea.' He climbed down the tree and sat by the acorn, feeling somewhat vexed.

By and by a hedgehog ambled along and saw Bramble scratching his head in frustration.

'Why, what's the matter Mr Squirrel?' asked the hedgehog, in her cordial hedgehoggly manner.

Bramble sighed, 'I found this lovely big acorn to eat,' he said, 'and I'm trying to crackle it, but it's just too hard!'

The hedgehog thought for a moment, 'There's a big old rock over there,' she said. 'Why don't you try hitting it on that?'

'Now that *is* a good idea,' said Bramble. 'Something more solid like a rock is sure to crackle it!'

Bramble pushed and shoved and rolled the acorn the short distance to the big old rock over there. Struggling under the weight, he somehow managed to lift the acorn and, heaving with all his might, throw it down onto the top of the rock. Again the nut just bounced off, almost hitting the hedgehog on her prickly head. Grumbling in a less than cordial manner, she trundled off into the hedgerow.

Bramble sighed once more and sat down on the rock with a furrowed brow, resting his chin on his paws whilst scrutinising the acorn.

Before too long a rabbit happened by, spotted Bramble sitting there deep in thought, and said 'Hello Mr Squirrel, you look as if you have the troubles of all Bunny Wood on your shoulders. Whatever is the matter?'

Bramble looked up at the rabbit. 'This blessed acorn is the matter,' he said. 'I've tried everything to crackle it, but it's just too big and too hard, and it's trying my patience let me tell you.'

'Mmm,' said the rabbit. 'It certainly *is* big!' He thought for a moment or two then said, 'Instead of crackling it why don't you try jabbing it with a sharp stick, and make a hole in it, like a weevil-thingy does?'

'A weevil-thingy,' said Bramble. 'Now that might just work. If tiny weevil-thingies can make holes in acorns then I reckon a big strong fellow like me can. Thanks Mr Rabbit.'

'Any time,' said the rabbit, pleased with himself for being so clever, 'Glad to be of help.' and hopped away down the path with a distinct air of genius.

Bramble looked around for a stick, found a sturdy one nearby, and set about sharpening one end with his hard squirrel teeth. Satisfied with the result, he grasped the stick firmly in his paws, raised it above his head and jabbed with all his might at the acorn. What, I suppose, do you think happened then? As you might well have guessed, the weevil-stick bounced off the troublesome nut and flew out of Bramble's paws.

The matter of the acorn was, by now, becoming too much for the hapless Bramble, who let out a squeak of despair, sat down with his head resting on the nut and began to sob.

Nearby, a woodland fairy was busy gathering fallen leaves with which to make herself a warm, comfy bed. Her sensitive fairy ears picked up Bramble's quiet sobbing. 'Someone's not happy,' she thought and, being a caring little fairy, 'I must go and see what's wrong.' She dropped her leaves and flew gracefully over to where Bramble was leaning against the giant acorn.

'Oh my!' she exclaimed. 'Such a woeful sight to see, I'm sure. What could possibly be the cause of such distress, you poor creature?'

Bramble looked up to see the fairy sitting by his side. He told her the sorrowful tale of the giant acorn and of his various attempts to crackle the wretched thing. 'So you see,' he said, 'there is all this food; enough to feed me for a week or more, and I just can't get at it!'

'Mmm,' said the fairy, that *is* a bit of a nuisance, isn't it? Let me think for a moment.' She sat on the acorn and pondered upon the problem. 'I do believe,' she said at last, 'that you're going about this the wrong way my dear squirrel.'

Bramble looked at her, puzzled. 'What do you mean?' He asked.

'Well,' said the fairy, 'If I help you to solve your problem, will you promise to share this lovely big acorn with me?'

Bramble had to consider the offer carefully, for he was not a naturally sharing kind of creature, 'Well,' he said, reluctantly, 'I suppose half is better than none at all, so yes; if you can help me to open it I'll share it with you.'

'Good!' exclaimed the fairy, rubbing her little hands in anticipation, 'Now, give me a hand to get this huge feast down to the lake.'

Bramble gave a kind of *'I suppose you know what you're doing'* shrug, and between them they began rolling the acorn over the path, through the carpet of leaves and down to the water's edge.

'Now,' said the fairy 'Go and peel me a nice, long strip of tree bark with your sharp teeth.' Bramble shrugged again, but did as he was told. In just a few moments he returned with a long, thin strip of bark.

The fairy took the bark, knotted one end tightly around the acorn's thick stalk, then flew up and tied the other end to an overhanging branch. 'Now help me to push it into the water,' she said.

Bramble gave her a look as if to say 'You're really quite mad, aren't you?' mindful of the fact that fairies have a reputation for being a little dippy from time to time. Nevertheless, he positioned himself alongside her and together they heaved until the acorn rolled down the bank and into the water with quite a splash.

The fairy stood, arms folded, regarding the acorn, which was now sitting just beneath the surface of the lake, held in place by the strip of bark, with a smugly smile on her face.

Still puzzled, Bramble said 'But it still looks the same to me. Did you expect the water to crackle it when tree stumps, hard rocks and pointy weevil-sticks couldn't? All we have now is a giant *wet* acorn!'

The fairy cast him a rather matronly sideways glance. 'You really must learn to have some patience my dear squirrel,' she said. 'Meet me here tomorrow, and then we shall see what we shall see.' With that, she waved goodbye and flew off to finish collecting her leaf bedding, leaving Bramble sitting there confused, and just a teeny bit annoyed, by the side of the lake.

Bramble sat up all night, keeping a watchful eye on the giant acorn in case anyone should try to steal it, which would be difficult as it was so heavy, unless of course, a night-bogle should happen by and decide it would make a tasty supper.

Fortunately, the night passed without incident and the next day, as promised, the fairy appeared, to be greeted by a very bleary-eyed squirrel.

'My!' she said. 'You look as if you've been up all night!'

Bramble squinted at her. 'Humph!' was all he replied.

'Very well, let's get on with it shall we?' said the fairy, grabbing hold of the strip of tree bark. 'Come on; help me pull this monster out of the water.'

Bramble yawned, stretched and reluctantly took a firm grip on the bark. Together they heaved and pulled and heaved again. Inch by inch they managed to pull the acorn up the bank and onto flat ground, where fairy, squirrel and the barely moveable feast finally came to rest.

Bramble was by now exhausted, what with the effort of tugging on the acorn and having had no sleep all night. 'I think I've had enough now,' he panted. 'Let's just leave this stubbornly old nut to the bogles. I'll go and scrump some normally sized ones before they're all gone.'

The fairy looked at him, smiling, and slowly shook her head. 'What did I say to you about having some patience, dear squirrel,' she said. 'Before you go, do you think you have enough strength left to try one more thing?'

'But I'm sooo tired,' pleaded Bramble. 'Just let me rest awhile, then I'll be on my way.'

'Of course, you must be exhausted,' said the fairy. 'Just you rest your head on this old acorn for a bit first and then you'll feel a little better.'

Bramble did as he was told. He crawled over to the acorn, sat down and rested his head against the hard nut; except it didn't feel quite so hard now. As a matter of fact the acorn felt softer; not like a fluffy pillow or anything, but definitely softer.

He looked up at the fairy, baffled.

'Go on,' she said. pointing at the acorn, 'Try your lovely sharp teeth on it now.'

Bramble turned back and tested the shell with his teeth. The all night soaking really had softened it!

With renewed energy, Bramble gnawed through the shell, and in no time had stripped it all away, leaving the wonderful nutilicious meat exposed at last. He was now so happy, and so awake, that he grabbed the fairy's hands, and they danced around in circles, all giddy and giggly.

Needless to say, Bramble kept his side of the bargain. Both fairy and squirrel feasted all day and into the evening; and what a grand repast it was, washed down with lovely elderberry juice, which the fairy had freshly squeezed that very morning. The little fairy even found that the acorn's cup made a perfect hat to keep her head warm in the winter and, as you might imagine, from that day on they were the best of friends; a model partnership of brains and brawn.

—— 3 ——

HOW THE FAIRY GOT HER WINGS

*T*here was once a fairy who was born without wings. Now this could be quite a hindrance to a creature that uses its wings to flit from one place to another, picking berries from high up in the trees or hiding from bogles, who often scoured Bunny Wood looking for unusual pets to keep locked up in cramped cages... or sometimes worse.

It should come as no surprise then that this particular fairy, let's call her Fae, as fairies tend not to tell strangers their names and, on the occasion that they do, are very difficult to spell, had to learn other ways of evading capture. Whenever warnings were sounded that bogles were around; panicky screeches and squeaks from birds, rabbits, squirrels and the like, most fairies simply took flight and hid in the higher branches of the trees.

Fae, on the other hand, was forced to take shelter in whatever nook or cranny she could find. Often this would be a rabbit hole, assuming she could make her way in before the doors were firmly shut and locked that is. Not that Fae was unwelcome in the rabbits' homes; indeed she was very popular among all the woodland creatures. The fact was that she could not run as fast as they could, and, believe me, a hasty retreat was everything when bogles were around. The day when she found herself locked out would be very worrisome indeed.

This particular warm summer's day began in the usual fashion; birds singing, rabbits munching away at dewy grasses and dandelion leaves, and fairies humming tuneful little ditties as they went about their business. Those of a more practical nature gathering brambles, elderberries and the like, while the younger ones, more disposed to mischief, playing 'tag' with the spring-born rabbits; tweaking their ears and flying off before finding themselves on the receiving end of a powerful bunny kick.

Fae, not being able to fly, had long since abandoned that particular game, after several bruising encounters with rabbit feet. On this fine day she was reclining on top of a toadstool, enjoying the antics of her young fairy friends as they swooped, tweaked an ear or two and flew off again. Before too long she had drifted off to sleep in the warm sunshine.

Suddenly, in the midst of the merriment, there was a loud shriek from above. Rabbits and fairies alike froze instantly, looking skyward to see Cornelius Crow swooping down from his nest high up in the trees.

'Bogle approaching!' he cried. 'Everyone hide! Quickly!'

In an instant there was such a flurry of activity. Rabbits hopping to and fro, the mothers and fathers calling their young ones home. Squirrels scampering up high into the trees. Birds taking flight, swiftly followed by fairies, at least those who *could* fly.

Naturally all this commotion woke Fae, who sat up on the toadstool rubbing her eyes, at first not realising what was happening. Then she heard Cornelius cry out again. 'Bogle! Get to safety now!'

Fae panicked, jumping down off the toadstool, looking frantically one way then another. The creatures had all but gone. She caught a glimpse of a rabbit's tail heading into a bramble bush and started to run after it as quickly as her legs could carry her, and she almost made it safely into the thorny tunnel; almost, but not quite. As the white fluffy tail disappeared into the bramble bush, Fae felt a tug on her legs, and before she knew it was pulled backwards, lifted high into the air and dropped unceremoniously into a dark sack.

After being jostled around in the dark for what seemed like ages; all sounds from outside muffled, so that she had no idea where she was, Fae eventually heard a creaking sound, followed by a loud slamming noise, before finally being dropped with a thump onto something hard. Then there was a faint glimmer of light as the sack was opened and a coarse, crackly voice spoke, 'Nah then, wot we gorreer?' A large, knobbly hand reached inside the sack and grabbed her roughly, pulling her out into a cold and dark room, lit only by a single candle.

Fae squinted in the dim light and confirmed her worst fear. Looking down at her was a sneering, ugly, warty face; a bogle! She instinctively tried to squirm out of the bogle's hand, but he just squeezed harder and yes, that would have hurt quite a bit let me tell you.

The bogle carried Fae over to an old table in a dark corner of the room, on which sat a cage made out of willow twigs.

'Eyupp!' croaked the bogle. 'Look at this. Why, it ain't gorenny wings!'

He opened a small door in the cage and threw her inside, shutting and securing it with a tightly-knotted piece of string.
As Fae lay trembling on the floor of the cage the bogle pressed his warty nose right up to the bars; so close that she grimaced as she caught a whiff of his rancid breath.

'Well I dunt reckon it's gunter be much fun as a pet if it dunt fly,' said the bogle. 'But I suppose it will make a tasty fuddle fer later on when I's feelin' a bit peckish!' With that he let out an ugly cackle and turned towards the door of his cramped, dark and dirty house. 'I'll sithee later,' he said. 'Dunt be goin' nowhere now, will thee?' Then he cackled again and left, slamming the door shut.

'A fuddle?' thought Fae, tearfully. 'Oh dear, I'm not sure what that is, but I don't think I'm going to like it. What am I to do?'

She got to her feet and looked around. As far as she could see in this dark and smelly room, she was alone. There were no windows; just a faint glimmer of light coming through around the edges of the door. Even if she could get out of the cage, there seemed to be no way of escape. She sat down, put her head in her hands and began to sob.

Presently Fae heard a scuttling noise. It sounded like something crawling around on top of the cage. She looked up and saw a big spider peering in at her with his eight beady eyes.

Fae gasped; for fairies, as with bogles and some other creatures for that matter, don't care much for spiders; don't ask me why, that's just how it is.

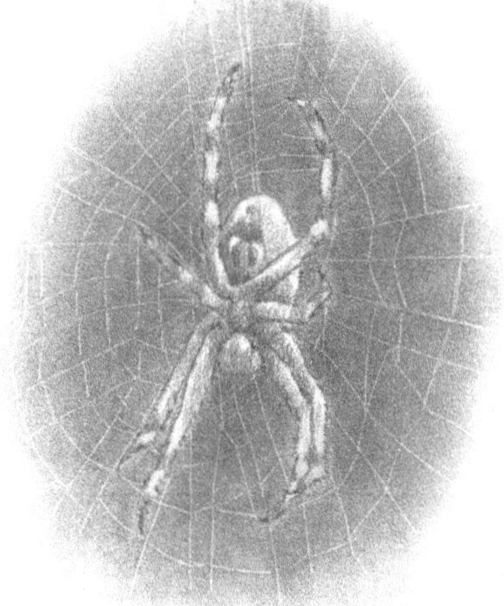

'Oh no!' cried Fae. 'First an ugly bogle, now a huge spiggedy-spider! Are you going to eat me?'

The spider cocked its head. 'Ah, a fairy is it? Don't be silly; spiders don't eat the likes of you!' It was indeed a fair-sized spider, but not so big that he couldn't squeeze its way between the bars of the cage, where he settled down beside her.

'I was just having a nice sleep up in my web when you woke me up with all that crying,' he said.

Fae shuffled away from the spider a little, still unsure of its intentions. 'I'm sorry to have disturbed you,' she said. 'But this horrid bogle caught me. Now I'm trapped in here until he comes back to make a fuddle out of me!'

'Oh dear,' said the spider, who didn't know what a 'fuddle' was either. 'That probably isn't a good thing is it?' He thought for a moment, scratching his chin with one of his legs. 'Tell you what, when the bogle opens the cage to make a fuddle out of you, you can just fly out of his reach, if your quick about it, and escape up the chimney can't you?'

Fae began to sob again. 'That's just it,' she said. 'I *can't* fly because I don't have any *wings*!'

'No wings!' exclaimed the spider. 'How can that be? All fairies have wings, surely?'

'Well, not *this* one!' said Fae, turning to show the spider her wingless back, 'And now I'm done for!'

'My, my,' said the spider. 'This is a bit of a pickle then isn't it?' He thought again for a few moments. 'Well, if you can untie that there string you can get out and climb up the chimney to escape before the bogle comes back. You can climb, I take it?'

'Yes, perhaps I could,' thought Fae. So she stood up and reached through the door, pulling at the knot as hard as she could. 'It's no use,' she said. 'The knot is too tight and I'm simply not strong enough!'

'Perhaps if we both try it together,' said the spider. So between them they tugged at the knotted string, but the bogle, being much bigger and much stronger, had tied it so tightly that it just wouldn't budge.

They both sat down, exhausted from their efforts. After a while the spider clapped his two front legs together and exclaimed 'I have it!'

'You have what?' asked Fae.

'The answer! The answer to all your problems!'

'Well then,' said Fae. 'Tell me, and please be quick about it, for the bogle is sure to be back soon.'

The spider motioned for her to sit down. 'Just you wait here Miss,' he said, 'I'll be back in a jiffy.' With that, he crawled through the bars, up the side of the cage and out of sight.

Fae sat down, leaning against the cage, for she could do nothing more. After what seemed an age, she heard the scuttling noise again, and the spider eased his way back into the cage.

'Well,' she said, despairingly. 'What am I to do?'

'My dear,' said the spider. 'You are going to fly out of here, that's what!'

Fae sighed. 'But I've already told you, I don't have any wings!'

The spider smiled smugly. 'Which is why I have made you these!' And with that he produced two shiny pieces of web and laid them down in front of her.

Fae looked down at the finely spun shapes, perplexed and a tad annoyed. 'I thought you were going to do something to help me,' she said. 'Not waste any more of the precious little time I have left spinning webs!'

'Now there's gratitude,' said the spider. 'These are no ordinary webs I'll have you know. These are the finest, lightest and strongest pair of wings that a fairy could ask for.'

'Wings?' said Fae, scornfully, 'Oh yes, of course they are. How silly of me not to have seen it!'

'Now, now,' said the spider. 'Don't be like that. Do you want them or don't you? Because I have other things to be getting on with you know, like sleeping and waiting for supper to land in my web.'

Fae sighed, 'I'm sorry,' she said. 'They are lovely wings I'm sure, but how am I supposed to use them?'

'Well, let's just see shall we?' said the spider. 'Now, if you'll just kindly turn around?'

Fae, by now, had become almost resigned to her fate. She reluctantly turned her back to the spider. Immediately she did so, she felt a tickling between her shoulders, and jumped a little.

'Hold still will you,' said the spider. 'I can't do this properly with you squirming around all over the place, can I?'

Fae gave a little shrug and then tried to keep as still as possible as the spider continued whatever he was doing behind her back.

'There!' said the spider after a few moments. 'All finished now.'

'Finished what?' asked Fae.

'Can't you feel them?' asked the spider.

'I can't feel any... wait a minute! Yes, I can feel something.' She twisted her head to look over her shoulder and caught a glimpse of the most beautiful, shiny silken wings she had ever seen.

'You might not have had any wings,' said the spider, 'but you have little stumps where they should be. All I did was to glue them on to those with extra strong silk. Now try to flap them.'

Fae could feel a tingling sensation between her shoulders. She closed her eyes and concentrated, trying to make her never-used muscles work. 'Is anything happening?' she asked.

'Yes,' said the spider. 'I can see them moving, but you'll need to keep trying. Those muscles will be quite weak remember.'

Fae concentrated even more. It was tiring, but she knew she had to make the wings work or she would never escape from the bogle's house. Her muscles ached and her head hurt from all of that concentration, but then, with one last supreme effort, she heard a whirring noise and looked over her shoulder to see the cobweb wings flapping so fast that they were just a blur.

'That's it!' the spider cried. 'They're working! Just a little more. See if you can lift yourself off the floor.'

Fae squeezed her muscles as hard as she could. They were aching now, but then the most marvellous thing happened. Just as she thought she could do no more, she felt herself being lifted off the floor of the cage; just a little, but, for the first time in her young life, she was actually flying!

Exhausted but joyful, Fae sat down and relaxed her wings. She still couldn't quite believe what had happened. 'Oh, dear spider,' she said. 'I really don't know how to thank you.'

'You can thank me later, when you're free of this place,' said the spider. 'You should rest now, but only for a short while mind you. You must keep practicing for when the bogle returns, so you can fly up the chimney when he opens the cage.'

Fae nodded and rested for a few brief moments before resuming her flying practice. By and by, with a lot of effort and quite a few short breaks, she was able to lift herself up in the air quite easily. How she would fare on a longer flight she couldn't yet know, as the cage was too small to actually fly around in.

It wouldn't be much longer before Fae had a chance to find out how well the wings would work, for just as she was having a practice, there was a loud creaking noise and the door opened. Quickly, she sat down with her back to the rear of the cage so that her new wings couldn't be seen.

The bogle came in, slamming the door behind him and walked towards her in that shambling, clumsy manner that bogles have.

Pressing his nose to the bars of the cage, the bogle sniffed. 'Eyupp my little princess,' he said. 'It 'as been a long day an' not much to show fer it. It looks like I's gunter 'ave to make do with a fairy supper this evenin' dunt it? And no crispy wings to chew on fer afters neither!'

Cackling away to himself, the bogle shuffled over to the fireplace, lit a fire under a large pot of water and threw in some rotting vegetables. Then he began to sing, somewhat tunelessly,

'Light the fire,

Boil the water,

Cook the fairy

Now I've caught her.

What's for supper?

Let's just see,

A fairy fuddle

Sounds good to me!'

Fae's heart was pounding. She knew that when the bogle came to take her out of the cage, she would have only a brief moment to make her escape, hoping that her tired muscles could make the wings work long enough to carry her out of his reach. She didn't have to wait for long, for the bogle, satisfied that the pot was ready, came back to the cage, an evil grin on his warty face showing his uneven yellowed teeth.

'Fuddle time I do believe,' said the bogle. 'Is thee feelin' peckish my little princess? I know I is!'

He reached out and began to untie the knotted string. Fae got to her feet, flexing her oh-so-tired wing muscles, preparing herself for her one and only chance.

The bogle had untied the knot and was now opening the door to the cage. He moved slowly, humming his awful song, for, as far as he was concerned, Fae could not fly, so there was no need for haste.

Then the door was open. The bogle leaned back slightly, admiring his supper-to-be. It was now or never. Summoning all the effort she could, Fae squeezed her muscles and felt the wings vibrating. Faster and faster they went, until she began to feel a lightness in her whole body. Her feet started to lift, unseen by the bogle. Fae took a deep breath and threw herself at the cage door.

That action caught the bogle by surprise, and he stepped back a little further, allowing Fae to make her exit, hovering just in front of his nose.

The bogle suddenly realised what was happening and made a grab for Fae with his huge, gnarly hand.

Forcing her muscles to work until they burned, Fae managed to evade the fast approaching hand, flying high above the bogle's head. She whooped out loud with joy, cast a glance down at his startled expression and made for the fireplace.

The bogle couldn't seem to work out what was happening, but still he turned and threw himself at the fairy, whose new wings were now buzzing, such was their speed.

As Fae reached the fire and flew above it, the heat from the flames and the boiling water actually helped to lift her even more, pushing her up the chimney.

The last Fae heard as she rose higher was a crash as the bogle landed in the fire, followed by a terrible screech as the cooking pot overturned onto him. Then she felt the heat from a shower of hot ashes following her up the dark chimney until, at last, daylight and she was free!

Fae allowed herself a moment to rest on the roof of the bogle's house, listening to his screeching and cursing. Then she took flight again. This time it was easier, for the warm summer evening breeze was beneath her wings, helping to keep her aloft. As she looked back she could see that the bogle's house had set alight from his collision with the fire. She feared for the spider, but there was nothing she could do now, even if she managed to get back into the house. 'Thank you dear, dear spider,' she said tearfully. 'I will never forget what you did for me.'

Towards the end of summer, at the height of berry season, Fae, now well-practised in the art of flying, her shiny gossamer wings the envy of all, was picking berries in a rowan tree. As she sat down on a branch to nibble at the delicious fruit, she noticed a spider's web attached to an overhanging leaf. She had, of course, seen many spider webs around Bunny Wood but this one looked particularly fine and sturdy

As she moved further down the branch to get a closer look, a big spider appeared from beneath the leaf. Fairy and spider looked at each other for a moment, and the spider said 'Well, hello there young miss. Those are, if I might be so bold, beautiful wings you have there!'

The spider smiled, and Fae, at first puzzled, smiled back.

'I do believe,' said the spider, 'that they must be the finest wings I have ever made!'

—— 4 ——

CORNELIUS AND THE EGG COLLECTOR

*I*wonder if you've ever walked through a wood and noticed egg shells of varying sizes and colours lying on the ground. Perhaps you have and not paid much attention to them; and if you did give them notice, you probably assumed they were shells from hatchlings, tossed out of the nest.

Well, the next time you see one of these shells, pick it up and look a little closer, for you may just find that the top of the egg has been neatly severed from the rest, as you yourself might do to a boiled egg at breakfast. That will be a sign that something rather unpleasant is going on.

Now there are several places around Bunny Wood Lake where birds nest and raise their young. There is Bunny Wood itself of course, where the rabbits live happily alongside blackbirds, sparrows, wrens and robins.

On the far side of the lake, in Pigeon Wood, it won't surprise you to learn, I'm sure, that pigeons make up the greater proportion of the bird population.

Of course, we mustn't forget the lake itself, which is home to the water fowl; swans, ducks, geese and the occasional visiting heron.

As well as all of Bunny Wood Lake's feathered residents, and more likely because of them, lived an altogether more sinister-looking creature; a not-too-handsome bogle, known to all as Beaky McSneaky.

Now, McSneaky was, to those who knew about such matters, a 'bird-bogle'; and a particularly unpleasant one at that. In some manner he resembled a bird, with a smooth, domed egg-shaped head and a large, pointed nose, giving rise to the first part of his nickname, 'Beaky'.

McSneaky's bird-like appearance was further enhanced by his coat, which was a tatty affair, being made up of hundreds of bird feathers, all now darkened and ragged with age, and spotted here and there with dried, unpleasant-smelling eggy stains. No doubt then that Beaky McSneaky was a very odious and unkempt-looking creature indeed.

As a rule, bogles do not work for a living; rather they let others toil, while they find ways to reap rewards from such labours. McSneaky himself was an egg collector. That sounds harmless enough you might think, until you realise that his purpose in life was to steal birds' unborn babies and eat them!

Beaky McSneaky was also a kind of tax collector, taking one from each clutch of newly-laid eggs around Bunny Wood Lake regardless of whether there were half a dozen eggs or just the one. This was his 'tax' on the bird population. If a bird refused him, he simply took all of their eggs and forcibly evicted them from their nest, which left them little choice but to meet his demands, especially as he was much larger than they were. In short, McSneaky was a bully; a sort of bird-bogle landlord who ruled the roost

Now it so happened that, one fine day in early spring, a new couple arrived to make their home in Pigeon Wood; a certain Cornelius Crow and his lovely wife, Cornelia.

There had never been a crow family around Bunny Wood Lake up until then. All of the other birds made the couple very welcome of course; showing them the best trees that were free to nest in, where the soil was ideal for digging up worms and so on. Then, of course, they regretfully had to tell them of the bird-bogle and his cruel 'tax'.

This worried Cornelia, naturally, as she was looking forward to having her first offspring in their new home. Cornelius, however, was less concerned, being the big, strong bird that he was. 'Just let that old bogle try it with me,' he said. 'I'll give him a taste of the sharp end of my beak!'

As the glorious days of spring rolled on and grew warmer, the birds of Bunny Wood and Pigeon Wood began to nest. Eggs were laid and softly sat upon. All kept a watchful eye out for thieves, especially the dreaded Beaky McSneaky.

Mr and Mrs Crow were blessed with their first offspring, and, even though it was but a single egg, Cornelius couldn't have been a prouder father-to-be; but Cornelia wasn't able to hide her concern that her precious egg might be taken from her at any time.

Before long the dreadful day arrived, when McSneaky began his first round of collecting. Most of the birds, especially the smaller ones, gave in easily. There was nothing they could do, as the bogle was too strong; but at least they were left with other chicks to hatch, and so, reluctantly, they each had to let one egg go.

The mean bogle continued his rounds, stashing eggs in the pockets inside his coat as he went, but also lopping the tops off some there and then with a sharp knife and guzzling the contents, yolk dripping down his chin and onto his raggedy, feathered coat.

Eventually he arrived at the tree where Mr and Mrs Crow had made their nest. Climbing up through the branches, he found Cornelia sitting on the nest, with Cornelius standing protectively by her side.

'What do we have here?' McSneaky croaked in a voice that was neither bogle nor bird, but somewhere in between. 'New tenants, eh? I'll wager you have some tasty eggs in that lovely nest of yours!'

Of course Cornelius was having none of it, this being their first born and all. As McSneaky reached out to push Cornelia off the nest and claim his prize, Cornelius lurched forward and pecked the bogle's hand as hard as he could and, being a crow's beak, that was a painfully hard peck let me tell you.

McSneaky screeched with pain and pulled his hand back sharply. 'You devilish creature!' he cried. 'How dare you do that to me! Pay me your dues now or I'll... I'll...'

Once again Cornelius launched himself at the bogle, this time aiming for his nose.

'Ow! Ow!' screeched the bogle. 'This time you've gone too far you crowbag!' He backed off and began to climb back down, issuing a new threat as he retreated, 'I'll be back tomorrow, and if I don't get my egg then I'll saw this branch off and you can wave your nest goodbye!' With that he left, grumbling and moaning about his sore hand and nose.

Cornelius couldn't help feeling a great deal of satisfaction for having seen off the bogle, but Cornelia was more concerned. 'Oh Cornelius,' she sighed, 'what are we to do? If that horrible creature comes back we will lose the nest *and* our baby!'

Cornelius wrapped his wing around her. 'Don't worry my dear,' he said, trying to comfort her as best he could. 'I'll think of something. That beast will not take our little one, I promise you.'

All night Cornelius stayed awake, guarding the nest and thinking. 'Something must be done,' he thought. 'It's not right that these birds' eggs are being taken just to satisfy that monster's greed.'

He made up his mind that, in the morning, he would call a meeting with all the birds around Bunny Wood Lake to discuss the problem and find a way to stop Beaky McSneaky stealing their eggs.

The next morning, before the sun was barely awake, Cornelius set off and flew all around the lake, calling each and every bird to an urgent meeting, to be held in a clearing in Pigeon Wood.

Shortly thereafter the clearing was filled with birds of every kind, from tiny wrens to enormous swans.

Cornelius sat on a branch looking down at the waiting assembly and cleared his throat. 'Firstly,' he began, 'thank you all for coming to this meeting.' The crowd began to chatter away to each other, wondering what it was all about. 'Secondly,' he shouted in his loud cawing voice, 'I know that my wife and I are new here, and we thank you for welcoming us into your community, but there is a stain on this otherwise peaceful place that needs to be removed.'

The meeting suddenly fell silent. 'I believe,' Cornelius continued, 'that you all know what, or rather *who,* that stain is.' Again, there was a loud chattering. Cornelius held up his open wings to quiet them down. 'Many of you, I know, have had to put up with this evil 'tax' on your eggs for years.' This was met with a low murmuring. 'Some of you have had your only offspring taken.' A hum of acknowledgements followed. 'My wife and I are expecting *our* first child, and I, for one, will not have that child taken and eaten before it is even born!'

There was now a hush, as if all of Bunny Wood Lake had fallen silent, hanging on to every word.

A pigeon cooed from the back of the crowd, 'Yes, you're right,' he called out. 'We have had to suffer this for many years. Some have been so heartbroken by their loss that they left their homes in the hope of finding somewhere safer.' The crowd again acknowledged this. 'But let me say this,' the pigeon continued. 'For most of the time, this is a haven for all of us, and there are simply too few places left where we can find food and shelter and everything else we need.'

The vocal agreement increased in volume, with shouts of 'That's right!' and 'Where else can we go?' and 'What else shall we do?'

Cornelius waited for the hubbub to die down, then raised his wings again, 'What you say is true,' he called out. 'I have lived in places where bogles have simply taken over, and where I certainly wouldn't want to raise a family. It is almost perfect here, except for one thing; and you all know what that is. We must rid ourselves of this egg thief, so we can be truly happy *all* of the time!' He looked down at the assembly of birds and was pleased to see many of them nodding to each other and to him in agreement.

'This is what we do,' Cornelius resumed. 'We have, together, great brain power; 'bird brain' power, and that, my friends, is a force for any bogle to fear; and by our brains shall we defeat him!'

Agreement with what Cornelius was saying was gathering momentum, turning into an array of shrill whistles, coos and screeches. He waited until they had settled down and said calmly 'Now, what we need is a plan.'

'Why not kill him?' screeched an old Greylag goose. 'There are enough of us if we all attack him together.'

A dove piped up, 'That is not our way,' he said. 'I am a bird of peace, not a murderer.'

'The dove is right,' said Cornelius. 'No killing. That will make us no better than a bogle. What we need is a deterrent; something that will make him leave and not come back.'

This last remark prompted all manner of suggestions, 'Peck out his eyes!' 'Bite off his fingers!' 'Cover him in poo!' This last remark provoked shrills and whistles of laughter. Then, as the noise abated, a soft un-birdlike voice said 'You have to be cunning with bogles.'

All the birds looked around to see who had spoken, until their eyes settled on a nearby branch where a grass snake coiled, looking out at the assembly.

'I see you have a problem,' hissed the snake, having the full attention of the birds. 'I do believe I can help you. Come a little closer, as I don't like shouting, and I will tell you what I have in mind.'

The snake outlined his plan, which met with great approval, especially from Cornelius who thought that here was a creature who was almost as intelligent as a bird.

The next few hours were spent in a frenzy of high-spirited activity putting the snake's plan into action. When eventually all was prepared, the birds went about their usual business, creating an impression of normality.

By and by Beaky McSneaky appeared and began to make his rounds, collecting eggs from those who had not yet paid their 'taxes'.

He started with a couple of pigeons who had not laid eggs by the first collecting day, but hoped they would have some by today. To McSneaky's delight, they had indeed and, from a clutch of three eggs, he took one and put it in a pocket inside his coat. Next, he moved on to a blackbird family and did the same thing, and so on until he had almost filled his pockets enough for that day's round.

Now it was the turn of Cornelius and Cornelia. McSneaky had come prepared, with a long sharp stick, with which to stab at any bird unwilling to move off their nest.

As McSneaky climbed up to the crows' nest he reached out with his stick. 'If you know what's good for you, you'll move off that nest and give me one of them lovely crow eggs,' he said, threateningly.

Cornelia began to sob, protesting loudly. 'But we've only one egg,' she said, 'and it's our first born. Please don't take it!'

Cornelius edged closer to his wife, beak poised ready to defend her.

McSneaky jabbed at Cornelius with the stick. 'If you don't move' he said, 'then I fancy it'll be crow stew for supper!'

Cornelius turned to Cornelia, 'I'm sorry my dear. Let him have what he wants. We can always have more children.'

'Now that's a sensible birdy,' said McSneaky, as Cornelia reluctantly moved off the nest and sat next to Cornelius on the branch.

The bogle was drooling with anticipation as he reached out for the solitary egg. 'This one is so special,' he said, 'I do believe I'll eat it right here while it's good and fresh.'

The bogle picked up the egg, took out his knife and began to cut off the top, planning to gulp down the contents, while Cornelius and Cornelia looked on. Once the top was removed, he lifted the egg to his mouth, grinning at the crows as he did so. 'Down the 'atch my dears!' he taunted, and tipped the contents of the egg into his mouth.

Almost immediately his expression changed to one of complete horror. Wide-eyed, he looked towards the crows and parted his cracked lips. As he did so, a small fully-formed grass snake wriggled out of his mouth, bit his bottom lip and slithered down inside his coat.

McSneaky screamed, not fully aware of what was happening. He reached into his coat to rid himself of the snake, but pulled his hand out quickly, screaming again as he saw not one, but five little snakes each gripping onto his hand with their sharp little teeth.

The terrified bogle shrieked and retreated down the tree as fast as he could. Then he ran off screaming and shaking his hand to try and rid himself of the snakes.

As Beaky McSneaky disappeared into the wood, Cornelius and Cornelia stood on the branch and began to laugh. Soon they were joined by other birds, who had been hiding and waiting for this moment.

Then the grass snake appeared, slithering along the branch.

'I do hope your children will be alright,' said Cornelius.

The snake hissed, 'They will be just fine. They know how to look after themselves from the moment they hatch, and I think the bogle will have plenty of painful bites to attend to before long.'

They were joined by a heron who opened his large beak and gently deposited an egg on the crows' nest. 'I do believe this one is yours,' he said to Cornelia. 'And, judging by the wriggling I can feel inside it, you are going to be proud parents very soon.'

The heron was indeed correct. A few days later Cornelius and Cornelia Crow were blessed with a son. A fine-looking son who would hopefully raise a family of his own one day without fear; for from that day on, Beaky McSneaky was never seen nor heard of again.

—— 5 ——

KING EDWOOD'S DECREE

*I*f you ever find yourself walking in a wood and look up into the trees, being careful not to trip over the twisted roots of course, you might chance upon a squirrel scampering along a branch or shimmying up and down a trunk. Many years ago, long before you or I were even thought of, squirrels could be seen much more often, even when they were sleeping, for they would rest and sleep on the ground among those very same twisted roots.

Such a practice was not without its dangers however, as you always needed to keep one eye open for night-bogles out hunting. Not the ideal recipe for a restful night is it?

At around the time we've just been talking about, there lived a tree. Not just any old tree mind you; this was King Edwood, ruler of all the trees in Bunny Wood and, so it followed, all of Bunny Wood itself.

King Edwood didn't wear a crown, nor was he even elected king by those that make such decisions. It was simply understood, by virtue of the woodland law, that the oldest tree in the wood is declared the king. King Edwood was very old indeed, and he had ruled Bunny Wood for many years, the previous king having been chopped down by bogles and turned into tables, chairs and firewood.

Now, as often happens with older creatures, be it birds, rabbits or even trees, they tend to become a little hard of hearing; or in King Edwood's case, a *lot* hard of hearing. Normally, being hard of hearing wouldn't matter too much to most of the creatures; there are other senses to help them along, sight and smell for example, as well as having family and friends to help out. Being the king and not hearing very well is a different matter however. Solving disputes, such as who has fishing rights in certain parts of the lake, or which birds could nest in which trees, can be difficult at the best of times. When the one making the judgement is unable to hear the arguments on both sides, then it is near impossible to arrive at a just and fair solution.

King Edwood's hearing was becoming so bad that one day, he knew, he would have to abdicate and hand over the role to a younger tree, a tree perhaps with far less wisdom; something which no-one really wanted to happen for, despite his hearing difficulties, he was well-loved and respected.

In the autumn, trees tend to sleep rather a lot more; they stop growing and shed their leaves to save energy for the long winter ahead. On one such fine, if a little cold, autumn day, King Edwood was having one of his long afternoon naps, dreaming of warm spring days far ahead, when something began to stir him awake. Of late it would have to be something extremely loud to wake him; thunder perhaps. But he could feel something; a tickling in his ear, somewhat irritating as you can imagine, especially if you weren't able to reach up and scratch it.

The tickling sensation went on, and King Edwood was becoming more and more irritated. 'What on earth is tickling my ear?' he cried out.

He was about to call out for help, when he paused. Something was wrong, he thought. No, not wrong, but different, but what was it?

The tickling in his ear continued, and King Edwood was again about to call out when he realised *what* was different. The wind! That was it. The cold autumn wind, which normally didn't bother trees, unless it was a very strong, damaging wind, was whistling through his branches, and he could hear it!

Then he realised that not only could he hear the wind, he could hear scratching sounds in his ear.

Of course, as is the case for any of us, King Edwood could not see what was happening in his ear, and that made him a little nervous. 'Hello,' he said quietly, and again was surprised to find he could hear his own hushed voice clearly, 'Who or what is in my ear? Show yourself.'

The tickling stopped, and all, except for the wind, was quiet again. King Edwood was beginning to think that this was perhaps a dream, and that he was still asleep, when he felt something crawling from his ear, along the side of his face and onto his nose. He looked down his large, knobbly nose and was surprised to see a young squirrel perched on the end of it. 'Are you real, or in my dream?' he asked the squirrel.

The squirrel smiled. 'Of course I'm real,' he said. 'But I can't tell you if I'm in your dream, because dreams are in your head, and I haven't got that far yet!'

King Edwood was puzzled. 'Well, if you're not a dream, how is it that I can hear what you're saying?'

'Because I'm talking to you?' said the squirrel, somewhat cheekily, as squirrels can be.

'No, no!' said King Edwood, becoming slightly confused. 'What I meant was I couldn't hear much at all before I went to sleep. Now I can hear the wind, and I can hear you!'

The squirrel cocked his head to one side, thoughtfully, before answering. 'Mmm. I think I understand now,' he said. 'While you were asleep, I've been clearing out moss, old leaves and all sorts of rubbish from that hole.' He pointed in the direction of King Edwood's ear. 'You see, I thought I might build a nest in it for the winter.'

King Edwood's voice boomed out. 'Make a nest in my ear!?' Then, realising he could actually hear, said, a little quieter, 'Do you know who I am, you little upstart? I am King Edwood, ruler of all Bunny Wood, and you want to make your home in my ear?'

The squirrel looked saddened. 'I'm terribly sorry your Royal Treeness, I had no idea. I thought perhaps I might be safer up here, out of reach of night-bogles. You see the rabbits have warrens to hide in. The birds can fly up out to safety. The ducks and geese can take to water, but we squirrels have nowhere safe to sleep.'

King Edwood mused royally over this for a moment. 'Mmm,' he said. 'As king of Bunny Wood, it should be my duty to keep *all* my subjects safe. Why did no-one tell me this until now?'

The squirrel shrugged. 'Perhaps they tried, but I suppose you just couldn't hear them.'

King Edwood grunted. 'Very well,' he said. 'Finish building your nest. Then, if you would be so kind, gather together all the creatures around and bring them to me. I have something I wish to say.'

The squirrel did as he was told. He finished clearing out King Edwood's ear, making a fine warm and safe nest. Then he went off to gather together all the woodland creatures.

King Edwood smiled contentedly. For the first time in a long, long time, he could hear everything; the wind, birds singing, frogs croaking, fairies laughing and playing among the toadstools, even the quiet dropping of autumn leaves.

Presently the squirrel returned, accompanied by a whole multitude of creatures, crawling, hopping and flying behind him.

When they had all gathered around among his twisted old tree roots, King Edwood began to address them.

'Loyal subjects,' he began. 'Today is a memorable day for me. Thanks to this young squirrel who has brought you here to me, I can now hear everything that's going on in my kingdom again.'

'Oohs' and 'Aahs' came from the crowd.

He continued. 'I have always tried to keep you safe here, and now I find I can do even more.' He cleared his throat. 'I have made a decree, to be upheld in woodland law, that henceforth any creature seeking a home above the ground, safe from bogles, shall be allowed to live in the ears of any tree, as long as they promise to keep said ears clean and tidy, so that whoever shall be king can hear and respond to your grievances.'

The decree was met with a loud cheer, and the squirrel jumped back onto King Edwood, climbing his way up to the freshly cleaned royal ear; his new home, which from that day on he kept meticulously clean, much to the delight and obvious benefit of all.

—— 6 ——

THE GOOSE WHO WALKED TO THE MOON

*H*ave you ever looked into the night sky, when the moon is big and round, and thought that sometimes it looks so big you could almost touch it?

Often, on such nights, the creatures that live around Bunny Wood Lake stay up to gaze in wonder at the moon, for it seems to have a strange, magical influence on everything it shines down on.

Sometimes the effect of a full moon is so strong it makes the woodland creatures and birds do odd things. If you happened to find yourself somewhere like Bunny Wood on a night like this, treading softly of course, you might see all manner of curious activities.

If you are lucky, you may well see a gathering of fairies hosting a moonlit ball. Fairies dancing with frogs, twirling round and round so fast that fairies and frogs alike, with frogs holding on tightly of course, take to the air above the silvery moonlit lake. And when the frogs get too heavy, they all drop into the water, fairies having to be ferried to shore on the frogs' backs so they can dry their wings out.

There was one occasion when some snails announced that they were going to have a race, which caused great excitement, as snails were not normally renowned for being high-spirited. A track was marked out and wagers were made. Unfortunately, the snails were so slow that by the time they had finished, it was almost dawn, and everyone had fallen asleep, so no-one knew who had won.

Birds also tend to act somewhat oddly under a full moon. Some of them mistakenly think because it's so light, that it is time to get up. They flit about in the branches, singing their hearts out for a while, before they realise that it is still night time and go back to bed, waking up more tired than usual at dawn.

On such a night, you may yourself have been awakened by a flock of geese flying noisily over your house. This is because they too are a little bit muddled up. Such is the power of the full moon that the geese all take flight and head towards the silvery disc without even knowing why; all that is except one.

You see, somewhere between the bogle village and Bunny Wood, there is a pond. On this pond there lived a goose who couldn't fly. It seems that her flight feathers never grew quite strong enough to get her off the ground.

Anyway, the goose had become used to not being able to fly, and was happy to spend all of her time either in the pond, or feeding on the lush grasses by the water's edge, as most geese are. She had everything she needed in the water or on the ground. That's not to say that she didn't sometimes envy the other geese when they all set off on their flights of fancy but, on the whole, she was content as she was.

Now, I say 'on the whole' because there were occasions when this goose *was* particularly envious of the others. Those occasions happened to be when the moon was full. Those magical, brightly-lit nights when she watched the other geese flying in formation, silhouetted against that huge, silver ball.

One night, one of those special nights when the moon was particularly big, so big that it looked like you could just reach out and touch it, the goose made a decision. She decided that, as she couldn't fly, she was going to walk to the moon.

The other geese were still asleep, and she knew that when they woke up, they would be off flying to the moon, a lot quicker than walking, so she was determined to get a good head start.

As quietly as she could, without disturbing the others, the goose set off on her journey, paddling across the pond, making as little splish-splashing as possible.

As she neared the far side of the pond, she disturbed a mallard who was trying to sleep in a reed bed. 'Where are you off to at this time of night?' asked the mallard.

'I'm going to the moon!' said the goose. 'Isn't it exciting?'

The mallard gave a disgruntled 'quack', muttered something about 'silly goose' and settled back down to sleep.

The goose reached the bank on the far side of the pond and waddled up onto a path. When she looked up, the moon didn't seem to be any closer, but she had only crossed the pond so far and, of course, she realised that it was actually quite far away.

Now the pathway led one way to the bogle village, absolutely to be avoided, and the other into unexplored territory, at least as far as the goose was concerned, where who-knows-what might live. She supposed it was a blessing, or at least the lesser of two evils, that the moon was in the opposite direction to the bogle village; so she shook her feathers dry and waddled on down the path towards the big shiny disc.

The goose hadn't got far when she heard a noise coming from a tree just above. She stopped and looked up to see a squirrel looking down at her.

'Hello squirrel,' she said politely. 'You startled me.'

'Hello back,' said the squirrel. 'Have you got lost?' he pointed behind her, 'The pond is that way.'

'Oh no,' the goose replied, 'I'm not lost. I'm walking to the moon.'

The squirrel looked puzzled at first then he laughed out loud. 'Walking to the moon? You're as mad as a March hare! You can't walk to the moon; it's far too far away!'

The goose held her head up defiantly, 'I can do whatever I choose,' she said. 'And I choose to walk to the moon.'

The squirrel almost fell off the branch laughing, 'Well,' he said. 'Don't forget to send me a postcard when you get there!'

The goose chose to ignore that last remark and carried on waddling down the path with her head held high.

The trees on both sides of the path were starting to get a little bigger now and more closed in, casting strange moon shadows on the ground.

The goose began hearing all kinds of unfamiliar sounds, and she was, if not quite afraid, a little nervous.

Just then a squeaky little voice called out, 'Hello night owl. Where are you off to?'

The goose looked around, but could see no-one.

'Up here!' the voice called.

The goose looked up to see a bat, barely visible against the dark branches, hanging upside-down above her head. 'Hello, 'she said. 'I'm not an owl, I'm a goose and, not that it's any of your concern, I'm walking to the moon.'

The bat giggled, squeakily. 'Walking to the moon? You can't walk to the moon, you silly goose!'
'And why not?' said the goose. The bat spread his leathery wings out wide. 'Do you see these?' he said. 'These are the finest and strongest wings ever made. Even flying, the sun would be up before I could get anywhere near the moon, and you think you can walk there?'

'Well at least it's better to try, rather than hanging around upside-down in a tree all night, don't you think?' said the goose.

'You must be as nutty as a squirrel!' replied the bat.

'Humph!' said the goose. 'We shall see what we shall see!' and, with that, she shook her tail feathers and walked on, leaving the bat giggling in the tree behind her.

Some way further on, the goose arrived at Bunny Wood Lake, which of course she had heard of but never visited. The lake was bordered here by bramble bushes. By now her feet were getting a little sore from all the waddling on dry land, and as the moon appeared to be just the other side of the lake, she welcomed the idea of paddling for a while.

Just then, there was a rustling sound from one of the bramble bushes and out popped a hare, dancing for all it was worth about the path in the moonlight.

'Hello,' said the goose. 'You seem happy.'

The hare turned to face her, hopping from one foot to another. 'Happy?' it said. 'Happy? Do I look happy?'

The goose studied the hare, who couldn't seem to keep still at all. 'Well actually you look... I don't know... a little strange?'

The hare continued to dance about with an odd look in its eyes. 'Do you know what it's like having this thing get you out of bed?' it said, pointing to the moon. 'Out of bed and dancing all night? Do you? Do you?'

'Well, I suppose not,' the goose replied. 'But I'll have a word about that if you like, as soon as I get there; for that's where I'm going. I'm walking to the moon.'

The hare stopped dancing just long enough to frown at the goose and say 'Walking to the moon? You must have bats in your belfry!' Then, without another word, it danced off under a hedge and into the field beyond.

The goose looked at the dancing hare as it disappeared into the field, 'And everyone thinks *I'm* bonkers!' With that, she jumped up, clapped her big webbed feet together and headed towards the lake.

When she reached the water's edge, the goose looked out onto a lovely still lake, much bigger than the small pond she was used to. At the far side, she saw the moon; as big and as shiny as could be sitting almost right on top of the water.

'Big, isn't it?' a little voice croaked.

The goose looked down. Sitting beside her was a big warty toad looking out across the lake.

'Oh hello,' she said. 'You mean the moon? Yes it is rather, isn't it?'

The toad cocked its head to one side, gazing wide-eyed at the moon. 'So big, you could almost touch it.'

'That is exactly what I intend to do,' said the goose.

The toad turned and looked up at her, frowning. 'I beg your pardon?'

The goose sighed. 'I have paddled, I have walked, and now I am going to swim to the moon!' she exclaimed. 'Isn't it wonderful?'

The toad turned back to gaze at the moon, thought for a moment and said simply,' You're as crazy as a box of frogs.'

'Crazy, am I?' said the goose. 'Well I'll show you! I'll show all of you!' With a hop and a skip, she jumped into the water and began swimming just as fast as she could.

When she reached the far side of the lake, where the moon was almost touching the water, the goose reached up and tried to touch it with her beak, but, despite all her efforts, she merely touched the air.

'Oh my,' she thought. 'Perhaps they were right after all. Maybe I *am* bonkers.' Then she sat there, floating on the water, looking very sad indeed.

At that moment a fairy happened by, on her way to a frog and fairy ball, and said 'Oh dear Miss goose! How can anyone look so sad on such a lovely night as this?'

Holding back a tear, the goose told the fairy her whole story.

After she had heard the goose's tale, the fairy smiled and said, 'But don't you realise? You *did* get to the moon!'

The goose sighed and thought, 'Well I suppose I'm not the only one who's bonkers, at least.'

The fairy spoke again, 'Just look down and you'll see. You didn't just reach the moon, you are floating on it!' Then she clapped her little fairy hands in delight and flitted off to the dance.

The goose, puzzled, looked down. All around her, as big as you like, was the moon, or at least the moon's reflection, but perfect in every detail on the still water of the lake.

'Yes!' she cried, 'I did it! Look at me!' she called out for all to hear. 'I'm on the moon!'

The commotion alerted all the creatures around Bunny Wood Lake. They looked out onto the water, and even the flock of geese from the pond, who were now flying overhead, looked down to see the goose floating happily on the moon's reflection, her feathers shining brightly in the silvery light.

From that day forward no-one, not the squirrel, nor the bat, nor the toad, not even the mad March hare thought ill of the goose, for she had indeed, in her own way, walked to the moon and fulfilled her dream.

THE HUMBLE RAGWORT

Tis a sight in summer to behold

And outshines all with blooms of gold

It prospers yet where many fail

On every hill, down every dale

Though most would call it 'noxious weed'

It still performs a goodly deed.

The moths and butterflies and bees

Whose appetites it doth appease,

Would prosper less if it were gone

Its nectar not to feed upon.

Its raggedy leaves are perfect food

For the cinnabar's stripy, hungry brood.

Ragwort fairies love them too

Its bitter leaves a medicinal brew.

So next time you meet this humble wort

Please try not to be too curt

Remember that, by nature's grace

Every plant has its rightful place.

— 8 —

SLIPPERY JACK

*T*hey speak of it on nights such as this, when the air is chilled and rain beats hard against the window. When the autumn winds howl through the trees around Bunny Wood, stripping them of their fading leaves. On nights when Bunny Wood Lake itself becomes a black hole under a moonless sky, by the safe glow of a warm fire, they tell tales of eerie melodies being sung out on the dark, cold waters.

If ever there was an odious bogle, then it was one who lived in a hole. The hole in question was half-hidden by old, bare branches by the edge of the pond at Bunny Wood Lake. If you were to walk around the pond and look across to the island, you would be hard-pushed to see it in daylight.

But if you dared to take the same route in the dead of night, you might well see a glow from a fire. And, if you looked closer, you might even spot a rather peculiar little figure squatting by the fire, upon which sits an old copper cooking pot. And, if you listened hard enough, you might just hear a strange, croaky voice singing.

Fire, cooking pot and croaky voice all belonged to a slovenly bogle, known to inhabitants of Bunny wood as Slippery Jack, a slimy, greenish-skinned creature who lived alone in the hole, rather like a hermit.

In the daytime Slippery Jack slept, hiding himself away from prying eyes. But at night time, when most creatures were asleep, his day began; for night time was the time when creatures of particular interest to him emerged. These creatures were frogs; and this bogle was by trade, if you could call it a trade, a 'frog-catcher'.

Slippery Jack absolutely loved frogs; not in a pick-them-up-and-cuddle-them kind of way you understand; more of a catch-them-and-put-them-in-the-cooking-pot kind of way. Every night, except in the winter months, during which time he hid himself away and lived off pickled frogs, he would set up his cooking pot and cast his net into the pond.

I suppose you might be thinking by now that every creature has to eat, even a loathsome bogle, and that there must be hundreds of frogs born every year, enough to go around surely?

You could be right of course, were it not for the fact that, in this case, Slippery Jack had simply grown too greedy by far. The time had long since passed when he would catch just what he needed to survive, plus a few extra to sustain him through the winter.

The frog-catcher now had an appetite for frogs far beyond what he needed. In fact the dozens of jars of pickled frogs he had stored away in his bogle-hole would have been enough for him to live on for the rest of his life.

The diminishing number of frogs on Bunny Wood Lake, caused by the greedy bogle, was creating a problem of another kind; disease-carrying mosquitoes, which happen to be one of the courses on a frog's menu. The more frogs that the Slippery Jack took, however, the fewer there were to control the mosquitoes; and that was making life troublesome for the general population.

And so it was on this night, a night like any other, the frog-catcher sat by his fire, cast his net and sang,

'Oh what a luvverly sight

In the middle of the night

To see the fire hot

Beneath the cooking pot.

Oh, what joy I get

Casting out the net.

What better than a fresh frog

Washed down with some tasty grog!

After a goodly amount of time, Slippery Jack had caught, cooked and eaten so many frogs that he had to lay himself down by the fire, picking his teeth with a bramble thorn, supping his grog and burping continuously. He tied the end of his net around his big toe so as to be alerted to a catch, because any frogs trapped in it, even now, were destined for the pot!

All of a sudden there was a tug on the net; not too hard a tug, but enough to make him sit up and take notice. Slippery Jack immediately thought that there might just be a big old frog in there and, if he couldn't manage to eat it now, it most certainly would end up in a pickling jar.

The next tug was a little harder. Now the bogle was sure he'd caught a big one. He untied the net from his toe and pulled. But to his surprise, the net, or rather what was in the net, pulled back.

Never one to turn down a nice big juicy frog, Slippery Jack braced himself and pulled harder. But, once again, to his even greater surprise, the net pulled even harder, almost lifting him up on his feet.

All went very still and quiet then. Slippery Jack stood up, wondering if his catch had slipped the net. He pulled again. There was something, he was sure of that, but this time it didn't pull back. Thinking that perhaps that big old frog had tired himself out, he went down to the very edge of the pond and looked into the cold, dark water, but could see nothing.

Just to be on the safe side, Slippery Jack tied the end of the net around his rather substantial middle, determined not to let go, and began to haul in his catch.

At first the net came up easily, then he could feel a little more resistance. He dug his heels in, leaned back and pulled with all his might.

All of a sudden the surface of the water broke and, for a brief moment, the bogle was both delighted and surprised in equal measure. It was indeed a frog, and yet it wasn't.

As his catch came up out of the water, Slippery Jack could see that it had the outward appearance of a frog, but much, much bigger. It was a giant creature, towering above him, its mouth open in a horrible grin, showing two rows of long sharp teeth which were very *un*-frog-like.

He gasped and thought, rather curiously, that he didn't have a big enough pickling jar. At that same moment the huge frog creature's head came down, picked up Slippery Jack, swallowed him whole and slid silently back into the water.

As you can imagine, when word went around Bunny Wood Lake the next day, there was great merriment; not only among the frogs but all the other creatures too.

By and by, the frog numbers increased while those of the mosquitoes decreased, which was of great benefit to the health of all concerned, I can tell you.

And to this day, if you happen to be around Bunny Wood Lake on such a night as this, and you listen carefully, you may just hear a plaintive, rather croaky voice singing from the depths,

'Oh what a terrible sight

In the middle of the night.

Never again will I feast

Trapped inside this fearsome beast,

Where all is foul and black.

Oh, woe is Slippery Jack!

—— 9 ——

THE CROW FAIRY

I'm sure you know by now that, as well as the usual woodland creatures, Bunny Wood is home to fairies. But did you also know that there are many different types of fairies, not just in Bunny Wood, but in woodlands everywhere?

Well, it's true, and it's because fairies, like any other creatures, evolve according to their lifestyle and where they live into a variety of forms, each with their own appearances, habits and abilities. If you happen to be out and about very early in the morning during spring and summer, you might well catch a glimpse of fairies with butterfly, damselfly or moth-like wings, such as the Burnett Fairy, with her red-spotted dark grey wings. Such fairies are quite common at that time of year, feasting on the same flowers as the moths and butterflies they take after.

More seldom seen are those fairies that only come out at night. You might spot them deep in the woods under the light of a full moon, flitting about with their bat-like soft leathery wings, but you would have to have very keen eyes to spot them!

Then there are fairies that live, mostly unseen by everyday folk, with birds of all shapes and sizes. Naturally, the wings of these fairies are feathered, which means that they can fly faster and higher than those with the gossamer wings of butterflies and moths.

Take, for example, one of the many types of 'bird-fairy' that lives in and around Bunny Wood, the 'crow fairy'.

As its name suggests, the crow fairy's habitat is high up in the trees, living alongside regular crow families. What distinguishes them and makes them easy to spot, for those who are prepared to take the time quietly observing, is their wings, which are black and feathery.

Young crow fairies will occasionally appear in a nest of new-born crows in the spring; a bit like a cuckoo in the nest but, unlike a cuckoo, she will not evict the existing occupants. On the contrary, she will become a part of the family and be raised by the crow parents exactly as if she were one of their own.

Anyway, once upon a time... oops! I should have used these words at the beginning, but never mind, I suppose this is the *real* start of our story.

So, once upon a time, not long after their first child was born, Cornelius and Cornelia Crow were out foraging for food for their hatchling. When they returned they discovered they had an extra mouth to feed; a tiny fairy, so small that she looked for all the world as if she had been hatched from the same egg as their own little one. Not that they minded in the slightest, for it was considered good luck, indeed an honour, to have a fairy move in with you. Besides, they both agreed, it would be nice for their son to have a sister.

As the weeks went by, the little fairy began to grow alongside her crow sibling. With her dark hair and feathered dress that her crow-mother had woven out of discarded baby feathers, for crows have especially well-shaped beaks for weaving, she even began to look a little crow-like in appearance.

Soon the pair would be out sitting together on the branch alongside the nest during the day. The fairy's feathery wings grew and strengthened, and it wasn't long before she was taking her first tentative fledgling flights with her crow-brother. The pair were inseparable, and they become known simply as Crow-sister and Crow-brother.

Now fairies, as I'm sure you know, are not all good all of the time. Neither are they all bad all of the time, but they can all be quite bad when the mood takes them.

This particular fairy was, shall we just say, rather naughtier than most, and in no time she was teaching her crow-brother to get up to all kinds of mischief in Bunny Wood, especially with a particular favourite game among fairies when they were being naughty, which happened to be dive-bombing bunnies and none-too-gently tweaking their ears.

It wasn't long before Cornelia grew tired of all the complaints she was receiving from the rabbits about her children's behaviour, so she rather sternly put an end to the ear-tweaking game. 'Why can't you play nicely, without upsetting anyone?' she said.

Crow-sister and Crow-brother sat together on the branch, in a bit of a sulk, wondering what they could play instead. By and by, after much hard thinking, Crow-sister had an idea.

'I know,' she said. 'You fetch one of those reeds from the water's edge and soften it with your beak. Leave the rest to me. Wait on that branch over there, and just do as I say when I give the signal.'

Crow-brother, as always, did as he was told. He fetched a reed, softened it until it was like a length of string and gave it to his sister. Then he waited on the branch while she flew off to do whatever it was she had planned.

Crow-sister returned and told her brother what to do. Shortly thereafter she signalled with a shrill high-pitched whistle. Crow-brother took to the air, flying low over the lake crying 'Bogle coming! Get in the water, quickly!'

Heads went up everywhere and all rushed to get in the lake; swans, geese and ducks alike. Three white duck sisters, asleep at the water's edge, woke up all of a fluster, and headed for the water, but ended up tripping and falling over each other, as Crow-sister had stealthily tied their feet together with the reed-string while they were sleeping.

The fairy and her brother's delight at this prank was short-lived as not only the three ducks, but all the other waterfowl complained noisily to Mr and Mrs Crow about their children's behaviour.

Cornelius apologised profusely, promising to seriously reprimand the children, who were forced to remain in the nest for the rest of the day.

The following day, Mr and Mrs Crow decided to allow the children to play out again, but made them promise not to perform any more annoying pranks.

Crow-sister and Crow-brother once again sat on the branch, wondering what they could play.

'I know,' said Crow-sister, with a distinctly naughty glint in her eye, 'Let's go cherry knocking!'

Now 'cherry knocking' was another favourite game among the naughtier fairies. It involved knocking on someone's door, usually rabbits and the like that lived in burrows, and then hiding just out of sight before anyone answered. Although generally a harmless, if somewhat annoying prank, you had to be very careful whose door you chose to 'cherry-knock', as there might be those who would not take too kindly to being unnecessarily disturbed.

'But we promised to be good, and not annoy anyone,' said Crow-brother.

Crow-sister smiled. 'We'll do it to Old Ratty,' she said. 'No-one likes him anyway.'

Now, Old Ratty lived by himself in a hole at the water's edge. No-one really cared much for him because he kept himself to himself, only leaving his house to scavenge for scraps of food. He would, and *could*, eat most anything on account of his long sharp teeth. He was also known for being a little bad-tempered, so parents warned their children from an early age to avoid him, and certainly not to annoy him.

Crow-brother hesitated, 'I don't know if we should,' he said. 'What if he catches us and eats us for his supper?'

'Don't be silly,' said Crow-sister. 'Even if he sees us, we're much too quick for him!'

Crow-brother reluctantly agreed, and so they flew over to the far side of the lake where Old Ratty lived.

The door to Old Ratty's home was a rickety old affair, made from twigs, with gaps in between through which, if they were not careful, they could be seen. Crow-sister decided to go first, knocking on the door and ever so quickly flying up onto the bank just above, where she and Crow-brother could look down to see what would happen.

Sure enough, Old Ratty opened the door. 'Yes!' he said. 'Who is it?'

When there was no answer, he stepped outside, looking to the left and to the right, and then down, but not up where Crow-sister and Crow-brother were looking down, stifling their giggles.

'Humph! Must have been the wind,' said Old Ratty, and went back inside.

'Must have been the wind!' Crow-sister sniggered. 'Go on,' she said to her brother. 'Your turn!'

Crow-brother took a deep breath and jumped down, standing nervously by the door.

'Go on! Go on!' urged Crow-sister. 'Hurry, or he'll see you!'
Crow-brother took another deep breath and rapped loudly on the door with his hard beak, then quickly flew back up to join his sister.
Again, Old Ratty opened the door with a more annoyed 'Who *is* it?' Looking left and right and down again, he could see nothing.
Nor, when he lifted his nose, could he feel the slightest breeze in the air.

'Humph! No wind. Someone is playing tricks,' he muttered. Then, more loudly, 'Woe betide whoever it is disturbing my nap! If I catch you... well, just wait and see!' With that, he went back inside, fair slamming the old twig door behind him.

Crow-sister and Crow-brother were in fits of giggles. 'If I catch you!' mocked Crow-sister in a deep, ratty kind of voice. 'This is much more fun than tweaking rabbit ears,' she said. 'My turn again, I think.'

'Mmm, perhaps we should stop now,' said Crow-brother. 'Old Ratty's getting really cross, and if he *does* catch us...'

'Woe betide!' said Crow-sister, again in her deep mocking voice. 'Don't be a scaredy-cat brother. Let me have one more turn, then we'll stop.'

Crow-brother was not too keen, but he agreed just to keep his sister happy.

Crow-sister rubbed her hands in delight and jumped down beside Old Ratty's door. She was about to deliver the hardest cherry knock of all when, along with a cry of 'Got you!' the door was flung open, knocking her backwards and into the water below before she was even aware of what had happened.

Crow-brother looked down, horrified to see his sister half-submerged and beginning to float away into deeper water, while Old Ratty, more than a little annoyed, shouted 'That'll teach you to disturb me!'

Neither Crow-sister nor her brother could swim and, as he saw her drifting helplessly in the cold water, Crow-brother panicked and began to fly around squawking, 'Help! Help! My sister is drowning! Someone please help!'

Under normal circumstances of course, any creature able to help would answer such a call without hesitation. However, when they saw it was Crow-brother, everyone ignored him, assuming it to be one of the pair's silly pranks again.

Crow-brother, now at his wits' end, looked down at his sister splashing about helplessly. Then, to his horror, he saw Old Ratty swim out and grab one of her wings in his sharp teeth, dragging her back to his hole, while all the time she was crying out and splashing frantically. Then the worst happened. Old Ratty pulled Crow-sister into his house and shut the door.

'Oh my, oh my!' cried Crow-brother. 'Now I'll have to tell mother and father what we've done, and my sister will be all gobbled up, and it will be all my fault for not stopping her!'

As fast as his young wings could carry him, Crow-brother hurried back to the nest and told his parents what had happened.

'Stupid children!' said Cornelius, angrily. 'What on earth were you thinking?'

'Oh, never mind the scalding now dear,' Cornelia pleaded. 'We have to go and rescue her from that horrid, dark rat-hole before it's too late!'

Cornelius and Cornelia set off with all haste, with crow-brother struggling to keep up behind them.

When they reached Old Ratty's house, Cornelius, big and strong as he was, wasted no time in pulling the door open. What they found inside Old Ratty's hole left them all speechless.

Far from being a horrid, dark hole, Old Ratty's home was very cosy-looking. There was a warm glow coming from a little fireplace off to one side. In front of the fire sat Crow-sister with Old Ratty beside her, preening her damp wings with a clump of dried grass.

Crow-sister turned to see her family gathered around, looking confused and perhaps more than a little relieved. She jumped up and hugged them all, one by one.

'I'm so sorry,' she said, sobbing. 'I thought I was going to drown for sure, but *Mr Ratty*' she emphasised the polite form, 'saved me!'

Old Ratty turned to face them with a warm smile on his face. 'I only did what anyone would do,' he said. 'Mind you,' he continued a little more sternly, 'I can't say I'm too happy at being disturbed while I'm trying to have a nap.'

Cornelius found his voice at last. 'How can I ever thank you?' he said. 'Rest assured they will be punished most severely!'

'Now, now,' said Old Ratty. 'I think they have been punished enough for their little prank, don't you? They are just children after all,' he said, smiling again. 'And children sometimes do naughty things.'

After that, the crow family and Old Ratty became the best of friends, always looking out for each other. When word got around of what he had done, Old Ratty soon became one of the most popular and well-loved of all Bunny Wood's creatures. Crow-sister and crow-brother promised never to be naughty again, and, for the most part, they were true to their word.

So, if you ever spot a rat by the water, minding his own business, don't think too badly of him; he's just trying get along as best he can, like you and I. And the next time you are out and about, especially in the spring, when woodland creatures are feeling playful and fairies feeling particularly naughty, don't forget to look up, for you just might be lucky enough to spot a little crow fairy sitting alongside a young crow, conspiring to start a new adventure. But that's a story for another time.

—— 10 ——

HORATIO THE HERON

Now the heron is a curious bird,
  Sitting hunched high in the trees.

And his tales seem often quite absurd,

  Of a life on the seven seas.

  He'll tell you of adventures bold

  Unchartered islands found.

  Of pirate ships and Spanish gold

  Buried deep beneath the ground.

  Of fishing trawlers lost at sea,

  To be seen again, no more.

Of mermaids, swimming wild and free

  Just beyond the rocky shore.

Of whales and monsters of the deep

  The Kraken, yet awaking.

Of Davy Jones, still sound asleep

Lost souls, his for the taking.

Oh, why then is he sometimes seen

At such a placid site?

Of all the places he has been,

A pond seems rather trite.

And should you ask, he would but say,

'Tis nought but a resting place.

When winter comes I'll be away,

With adventures new to face'

Which is why, when east winds blow,

And snow lies on the ground

This heron, called Horatio

Is nowhere to be found

—— 11 ——

THREE WHITE DUCKS

*I*n a quiet corner of Bunny Wood Lake, amongst a patch of lovely yellow irises, lived three maiden ducks; sisters actually. No-one knew where these gangly white-feathered ladies came from, and the other ducks and geese paid them little heed. They seemed to have always been there, largely unnoticed amid the more colourful waterfowl.

The sisters generally kept themselves to themselves, getting along for the most part, with just the occasional bickering, the same as siblings everywhere I suppose.

 As time went by and the sisters got older, they began to grow more and more jealous of other female ducks who were busy having families. Each spring they would watch with envy as eggs were laid and ducklings hatched, soon to be swimming in ordered columns behind their parents.

At moments like this, the three sisters would huddle close together and watch the flotillas of fluffy babies parading up and down the lake, all dewy-eyed, with 'oohs!' and 'aahs!'.

'We must have children of our own,' said the first. 'Before we're too old,' said the second.

'We need to find husbands,' said the third. And, as quickly as that, a decision was made.

The only problem was that there was currently a distinct shortage of eligible bachelors on Bunny Wood Lake; in truth there were none.

Very occasionally, however, new drakes *did* arrive at the lake, looking to find themselves a little home in a reed bed and perhaps settle down with a wife and family.

The sisters were aware of this of course. They had been living on the lake long enough to have seen all sorts of comings and goings, and so were prepared to bide their time a little while longer.

Then, one fine summer's day, there was a general commotion among the duck population. A new mallard drake had arrived.

'Most handsome! Very eligible!' was the news on the grapevine.

Now, the male mallard is a singularly handsome duck, with shiny blue-green plumage about the head, mustard-yellow bill and all topped off with a pure white collar around his neck. And it just so happens that female ducks take a particular fancy to brightly-coloured males, like our new arrival for example.

The new mallard wasted no time in attracting a following of female admirers, being quite the showy type with his particularly colourful plumage. He'd secured himself a fine, sheltered spot among the reed beds and was on the lookout for a wife to set up home with. Naturally, all of this hadn't gone unnoticed by the three sisters.
'Have you seen him?' said the first.

'Very fanciful!' said the second.

'Pity there's only one of him,' said the third.

This last statement suddenly took the edge of their excitement.

What they had hoped was for each of them to find a husband so that they could *all* marry and raise families together. Wouldn't that be just perfect?

'Mmm,' said the first.

'What to do?' said the second.

'Better one than none,' said the third.

With that, another decision was made. They decided that they would each present themselves to the new mallard and let him choose which one, if any, was to be his bride. The two not chosen would contend themselves being bridesmaids.

All three being in agreement, they pulled reeds to see who would be first to visit the drake.

'Me first!' said the first sister, having pulled the longest reed.

'Me second!' said the second, having pulled the second longest.

'And I have the short straw,' said the third sister, a little despondent.

That evening passed with much preening; each of the sisters trying to smooth down any ruffled feathers and appear as spotlessly white as possible.

The following morning, the first sister prepared to visit the mallard. 'Wish me luck my sisters!' she said, excitedly. This was followed by some indistinctly muttered phrases, which *could* have included the words 'good luck', but somehow I doubt it.

And so the first sister made her way across the water to the mallard's new home.

'Good morning sir,' she said, as graciously as she could.

The mallard looked her up and down. 'Good morning back,' he said, with a somewhat pompous air. 'What can I do for you madam?'

The duck replied, a little nervously, 'Well, as you're new here, I thought it only polite to make your acquaintance and perhaps we could, erm... well...'

'Spit it out now!' said the mallard, 'I have a lot to do today. We could what?'

The duck took a deep breath and said, 'Perhaps we could get to know each other a little better?'

The mallard laughed. 'You are seeking a husband I think!'

The duck, rather shyly, replied. 'Well, yes, as it happens, I am. Are you by any chance seeking a wife?'

'Well,' said the mallard 'I do find myself in a position to take a wife. As you can see, I am preparing a home fit for a queen.' He leaned a little closer, causing the duck to blush a tad. 'Tell you what. I'll set you a task. Bring me a gift, the *one* thing you love most, that means more to you than anything else, and I'll consider a proposal.' Then he raised himself up and puffed out his breast. 'Be off now, for I am extremely busy.'

This was more than the duck had expected. She was suddenly fidgety with excitement, and hurried back to her sisters to tell them the news.

On the way, she mused over her task. 'The *one* thing I love most?' she thought. 'I love my sisters more than anything else, but they are *two*! What am I to do? I can't possibly choose one over the other, or can I?' Then she had an idea. 'I know! I'll wait to see which one is the happiest for me and she will clearly then be the one I love most!'

When she returned, the first duck told her sisters that the mallard had set her a task, and if she performed it, he would likely marry her; but she didn't reveal to them what the task was.

'Oh sister,' said the second. 'I'm so happy for you!'

'Me too,' said the third. 'I'm so looking forward to being a bridesmaid!'

They each hugged her with such affection that the first sister realised she loved them both equally.

'Thank you my dears,' said the first sister. 'But I cannot marry him; the task is too hard for me.'

So, with the first sister's blessing, the second sister made her approach to the mallard. Once again, he set her the same task.

On her way back, the second sister realised that, despite their occasional bickering, she loved both her sisters equally.

'He is indeed most handsome,' she said tearfully. 'But I cannot marry him, for I too cannot complete the task.'

The third sister, by now suspecting that something was amiss, quizzed the other two about the task that the mallard had set. When they told her, she lifted her head proudly. 'Well, it falls to me now my sisters,' she said. 'This time I would like you both to come with me.'

The three ducks, led by the third sister, approached the mallard, who was busy preening himself.

'Well, well,' said the mallard. 'This is a nice surprise. Three lovely ladies come to court me!'

The third sister spoke up, 'My two sisters here have decided that they cannot complete your task. I am here to see if *I* can do better.'

'I see,' said the mallard. 'Well then. If *you* can bring me the one thing you love most, the thing that means more to you than anything else, I will consider a proposal of marriage.'

The third sister wasted no time in replying, 'The one thing that means more to me than anything else is loyalty,' she said. She motioned towards her slightly puzzled sisters, 'These two are what I love most in the whole world,' she said. 'Each of them rejected you because of their loyalty to and love for the others.' She stretched her neck so that she was eye to eye with the mallard. 'I would rather spend my life with my two loyal sisters than with a pompous old drake like you. So now *I'm* rejecting *your* proposal.'

With that she turned and beckoned her sisters to return to their own little home, leaving a rather deflated mallard behind.

From that day forward, the three sisters vowed that they would stay together, unmarried, and offer their services as nannies to any of the other ducks needing a break from their parental duties. They soon became the best-loved, if a little strict at times, 'aunts' on all of Bunny Wood Lake, and each season's ducklings were the better behaved for it.

As for the rather pompous mallard? Well, his ego having been somewhat dented, he left Bunny Wood Lake shortly thereafter and was never seen again.

—— 12 ——

SESSILE AND THE OAK TREE

Sessile was very fond of acorns, as most squirrels are. Now acorns, as I'm sure you know, grow from oak trees, and the thing is that there just aren't that many oak trees around these days; so Sessile was very fortunate indeed to find one when she first arrived in Bunny Wood.

The oak tree that Sessile made her home in wasn't *exactly* in Bunny Wood, but rather on the border; close enough I suppose you might say, but on the other hand... well, let's not get ahead of the story.

Sessile's tree turned out to be the perfect home not only for her, but for all manner of insects and birds too. Each autumn there would be acorns aplenty; so even if food was scarce in other parts of Bunny Wood, the oak tree and Sessile, being a generous soul, made sure that no-one went hungry over the long, cold winter months.

There was just one problem in this otherwise perfect arrangement, and that was where the oak tree had made *its* home.

Many years before, perhaps before you and I were even thought of, this particular oak tree was born from a single acorn that had been carried for some considerable distance in a crow's beak. The fields which bordered Bunny Wood on which it had taken root were really quite wild. Many different creatures made their homes in the surrounding lush meadows. Rabbits and field mice thrived on succulent grasses and dandelions. Bees, butterflies and moths delighted in the heady nectar of ragwort and wildflowers of such variety and beauty. Birds nested in fruit trees, crab apple, elder and the like, and grew strong on the plentiful harvest.

As the oak tree grew taller and stronger over time, the surrounding fields and meadows steadily began to disappear, giving way to ramshackle bogle dwellings.

Bogles, once confined to small groups along the edges of dense woodland, had grown too many in number. Where once they had cut down the occasional tree with which to build their dwellings, they now destroyed whole forests to build huge towns, and cleared meadows to create roads for their big, clumsy carts. Mother Nature herself was finding it harder and harder to provide for all the creatures that had depended on her since the time before the bogles arrived.

When Sessile first made her home in the oak tree, there were already settlements to the north and south of Bunny Wood. To the west, where meadows once flourished, were now wastelands where few creatures could live; a sure sign that bogles were getting ever nearer.

Now that autumn had arrived, acorn gathering was in full flow. Sessile had her own storage space in a hole in the oak tree, which was large enough to hold enough acorns to feed her through the winter; and there were plenty left over on the tree for all the other squirrels, mice and birds that lived in Bunny Wood to take and store.

Then one day, during the harvest, something happened that sent all the creatures who were hard at work into a panic, running this way and that away from the oak tree. A bogle appeared from the wasteland, pulling a noisy, rickety old cart behind him. As the shabby-looking figure drew ever closer to the tree, Sessile clambered up to the highest branches and hid herself, keeping perfectly still while she watched to see what he was up to.

The bogle stood for a moment, eyeing up the oak tree. Then from the cart he took out a huge axe and began to chop away at one of the lower branches. Sessile was horrified to see the home she loved so much being mutilated, and she couldn't help but screech loudly. The bogle stopped chopping and looked up, wondering where the noise had come from. He squinted, and then he caught sight of Sessile. 'Ha!' he exclaimed. 'A filthy little tree-rat!' He stepped back and shouted up, 'Oi, tree-rat! If I was you I'd get thee self off! I is 'avin this 'ere tree, and there'll be nowt left of it in a couple of days!'

What Sessile did next was simply audacious. Fearlessly, and without thought for her own safety, she ran down the tree at full speed and launched herself at the bogle's face, scratching his cheek and sinking her sharp teeth into his ear.

The bogle screamed with pain, waving his arms around furiously trying to rid himself of his assailant.

After a brief but fearsome tussle, Sessile jumped onto a branch, well out of the bogle's reach and watched as he retreated hastily to his cart, still screeching from the wounds inflicted on him.

'Now you've gone and done it!' he cried. 'Oh yes indeed! Just you wait you 'orrid little tree-rat! Don't go thinking as you've got the better of me, oh no!' He threw his axe into the cart and began to pull it back into the wasteland.

'I'll be back tomorrer,' he shouted back. 'There'll be more of us, and you 'ad better be gone or else it's a tree-rat fuddle for supper, mark my words, oh yes!' With that he trundled off, muttering 'Ow! Ow!' until he was out of sight.

Meanwhile, some of the other creatures had heard the kerfuffle and after the bogle had gone, came to see what it was all about.

Sessile, a little shaken, explained what had happened and told the others of the bogle's plan to return the next day with help to cut down the oak tree.

'Oh my!' said a rabbit. 'How brave you are Sessile. I don't think I could have done that!'

'Me neither!' a blackbird piped up.

'Nor me!' said a duck who had waddled over from the lake. 'Bogles are very dangerous creatures you know. Perhaps it would be better to leave them to it and find somewhere else to live.'

Sessile sat defiantly on the now-scarred branch. 'Never!' she said. 'This is *my* home and the food that this tree provides belongs to us. To me and you. To your children and your children's children.

When the bogles come back I'll be waiting for them, and I will fight them...to the death if I have to!'

Needless to say, Sessile slept fitfully that night. How was she, one little squirrel, going to defend her oak tree against who knows how many bogles?

Morning arrived rather quicker than Sessile would have hoped, and she still had no idea of what to do when the bogles turned up.

Well she didn't have to wait too long for, while the sun was barely awake, she heard a commotion coming from the wasteland.

Sessile scurried to the top of the oak tree and looked out to see not one, but half a dozen bogles armed with saws and pulling two big carts, big enough to carry away a whole tree, without doubt.

Quickly Sessile gathered as many acorns as she could from her store and made her way down to a lower branch, just out of reach of the loathsome creatures.

As the bogles gathered around the oak tree, the one from the day before, now with a deep welt on his cheek and wearing a grubby bandage over his ear, shouted up, 'Oi there tree-rat! I sees you ain't heeded my warnin!' He turned to his bogle gang and sneered. 'This is the devil what done this to me,' he said, pointing to his ear. The other bogles looked at each other and sniggered.

'Wot?' said one. 'You mean this ugly little tree-rat done that to a fine, strappin' thing like yerself!'

The bogles all laughed out loud, except of course the injured one. 'You go on and 'ave your fun!' he said. 'But these tree-rats is vicious little devils, let me tell you!' Then he turned back to Sessile. 'We is choppin' down this old tree 'ere whether you likes it or not! And you is goin' to be a right tasty supper and no mistake!'

The bogles paired up with the saws and positioned themselves to begin sawing away at the trunk of the old oak.

Sessile again acted without thought for her own safety, and began throwing acorns at the bogles as hard as she could. The trouble was, as she soon discovered, that the acorns, though hard, were too small to hurt such large creatures and they mocked her with false cries of 'Ouch!' and 'Ooh, that almost hurt!' and 'Be careful tree-rat, you'll 'ave someone's eye out!' Then they laughed their horrid bogle laughs and carried on sawing at the tree.

Now in despair, Sessile knew there was only one action left to her. She prepared to launch herself at the bogles, using her sharp claws and teeth again, knowing that it would likely be the end of her, when, all of a sudden, there was an almighty uproar. She looked over to the east, in the direction of Bunny Wood, and couldn't believe her eyes. The air was full of birds of all shapes and sizes. Marching and waddling over the pathway came ducks, geese and the mighty swans. Emerging from the bushes and undergrowth came rabbits, squirrels, even tiny mice, all screeching, cawing and chirruping so loudly as to make the worms pop their heads out of the damp earth to see what was going on.

The bogles stopped sawing and turned, covering their ears with their warty hands because of the noise, wondering what on earth was going on. There was little time for them to fully understand what was happening for, before they could begin to think about defending themselves, they were set upon by a huge mob coming at them from all directions.

Sessile looked on in amazement as, within a matter of a few seconds, the bogles were fleeing back to the wasteland, the air full of high-pitched screams in response to the various injuries inflicted by teeth, claws and beaks of the pursuing horde.

In no time at all the bogles were out of sight completely, but their cries could still be heard. The creatures of Bunny Wood returned triumphantly. All that remained of the bogles' presence were their saws and the two abandoned carts.

The victorious pack of assorted creatures gathered themselves around the base of the oak tree, cheering, jumping and flapping wings. When the hubbub quietened down, Sessile stood proudly on the lower branch and spoke out.

'My dear friends,' she began. 'I don't know how to thank you. What you did here was so courageous. You saved my... no... *our* tree and gave those bogles something they won't forget in a hurry.'

The crowd all voiced their agreement as one and, of course, they *were* now one; one big family who had learned that, together, they could accomplish anything. They had indeed saved the oak tree and its valuable harvest; for the bogles, to this day, never returned.

By and by the scars on the tree healed, but the memory of that day lived on through the generations that followed.

As a mark of respect, from that day on, a goodly amount of the annual acorn harvest was saved and distributed around the borders of Bunny Wood and beyond so that, in time, there would be many more oak trees providing food in plenty for all of Mother Nature's creatures.

—— 13 ——

MR SQUIDGELY IS STUCK

*I*t is well-known that squirrels need to eat a lot in the autumn in order to fatten themselves up for the coming winter, when food is scarce.

In autumn there are plenty of acorns and brambles around Bunny Wood for squirrels like Mr Squidgely to feast on; but, of course, they also have to store even more to last through until spring.

Mr Squidgely, in common with all other squirrels, had his own secret hiding place for his winter store. Some Squirrels like to bury acorns in secret places only they know; digging them up as and when needed. Mr Squidgely thought that this approach was a tad wasteful, as squirrels – clever as they are – couldn't possibly remember where *every* buried acorn treasure was. This was Mother Nature's plan of course. Acorns that were forgotten by spring were either dug up by birds, eaten by insects or, surviving all that, would eventually grow into new oak trees which, in turn, could feed even more woodland creatures.

But no; Mr Squidgely, being a thrifty sort, hated the notion of wasting even one acorn that he had so meticulously harvested and so had his own pantry where each and every nut was accounted for.

Mr Squidgely's acorn pantry was inside a hollowed-out tree, long since passed away, and the only access was through a hole which used to serve as the tree's ear. So, all through the autumn, he gathered in as many acorns as he could find and deposited them right down inside the base of the old tree.

Now it happened that this particular season had produced a bountiful crop indeed. There was a great deal of squirreling to and fro, I can tell you. Acorns were buried and stashed all around Bunny Wood, and it looked for certain as if no-one would go hungry that winter.

Mr Squidgely, as well as feasting like never before, had a pantry full of acorns that would have seen a whole family of squirrels through the winter by the time the harvest was over.

As the first icy winds blew in from the east, the squirrels of Bunny Wood were already spending more time in their nests, keeping warm and eating well; venturing outside only on milder, sunny days after the early hoar frosts had melted away for a little exercise.

Mr Squidgely, on the other hand, decided that he was far too warm and cosy inside the hollow tree and besides, it was the feasting season after all, and he had a huge pile of acorns to get through before spring. And get through them he did! In fact he spent the whole winter tucked up in his den eating and sleeping, without once going outside.

When the first buds of spring arrived in Bunny Wood, Mr Squidgely had but one or two acorns left, but that didn't matter as there would be catkins, flowers and bulbs aplenty waiting for him outside.

With a yawn and a stretch, he made his way up the inside of the hollow tree. He was looking forward to being out in the spring sunshine and exercising for the first time in months, especially as he was feeling particularly sluggish.

Mr Squidgely reached the entrance to the den and popped his head out, taking in the wonderful scents and pleasantly warm sunshine of early spring. Yes, it was indeed a lovely day for getting out and about and stretching his legs, somewhat stiff from being cooped up in his den all winter. He put his two front feet on the lip of the hole and pushed up with his back legs. And then what do you think happened? Well, he managed to squeeze his head and front legs out of the hole, but that was as far as he went. It seemed that he had simply put on too much weight over the winter months. He decided to withdraw and try again, except now he found that he couldn't get back into the hole as his elbows were in the way, and he could progress neither forward nor backward.

Again and again he tried pushing and pulling until he was exhausted, but it was no use; Mr Squidgely was stuck!

'Oh bother,' he thought. 'Now what am I to do?'

Just then a Magpie happened to land on a branch close by, and he couldn't help but notice Mr Squidgely, with his head poking out of the hole. 'Good morning to you!' he called, 'What an especially lovely day. Are you on your way out somewhere?'

'Oh dear,' thought Mr Squidgely. 'How embarrassing!' He forced a smile and replied, 'Oh yes, I am. I thought I might just rest a while here first and take in a little sunshine.'

'Good for you,' said the Magpie. 'Anyway, busy, busy, busy! Lots to do! Enjoy your day!' With that he flitted off through the branches, chattering away happily.

Mr Squidgely tried again to pull and push his way out of the hole, but to no avail. Oh why did he eat so many acorns? Or at least why didn't he follow the example of the other squirrels and exercise more over the winter?

And so he hung there, wedged tightly, contemplating his woes and wondering how long it would take to lose some of his excess padding. Presently, Bramble, another squirrel he was acquainted with, caught sight of him from a neighbouring oak tree.

'Good morning Mr Squidgely!' Bramble called out. 'I haven't seen you all winter. What are you up to this fine morning?'

Mr Squidgely dearly wanted to tell him that he had eaten far too much and was completely stuck, but he felt a little ashamed of himself, especially when he saw how trim and spritely Bramble appeared.

'Oh,' he said.' I feel the cold rather too much nowadays, so I didn't go out very often.' It wasn't exactly the truth of course, but what was he to say?

'Well, it's a lovely day today,' said Bramble. 'Why don't you join me? I'm off in search of catkins for breakfast.'

The mere thought of eating now made him feel queasy, even if he *could* get out. 'Oh, I think I'll just take it easy today,' he said. 'Perhaps tomorrow?'

'Suit yourself,' said Bramble, 'But I'm famished. Bye for now!' Then he was off, leaping from branch to branch in search of his catkin breakfast.

Mr Squidgely wished he had had the courage to tell Bramble of his predicament; he might even have been able to help him. Who knows how long he would be stuck here now?

As the morning went on, all manner of woodland creatures came and went; each full of the joys of spring. Mr Squidgely passed the time of day with those that stopped to chat, but still couldn't bring himself to explain his situation or ask for help.

By and by all went quiet around Bunny Wood, as it was now early afternoon, and time for snoozing; except for Mr Squidgely, who was far too troubled by the pickle he was in to sleep.

In the stillness he heard a sound above his head, a faint tapping noise that might otherwise be muffled by the general hubbub. Not able to tilt his head up to look for the source of the tapping, Mr Squidgely called out.

'Who's that, tapping away?' he asked. 'Can't you see I'm trying to have a nap?' Of course, he was still trying to hide the fact that he was stuck.

A tiny voice answered, 'Oh, I'm very sorry, but it is quite an unusual position for having a nap, isn't it?'

Mr Squidgely cleared his throat. 'Humph! It may well appear that way,' he said. 'But I happen to find it comfortable. Anyway, who are you? Show yourself.'

Then he heard a quiet scuttling sound around his head, and presently a small creature came into view.

'Oh squirrel, sir. Please forgive the intrusion,' said the tiny creature. 'I am but a humble wood-beetle looking for something to nibble on. Is this your tree?'

'As it happens,' said Mr Squidgely, 'it is my *home*.'

The wood-beetle looked at him, then scurried around the hole above, below and both sides of Mr Squidgely. Then, facing him again, said, 'You're stuck, aren't you?'

'No, not at all!' came the somewhat indignant reply. 'I don't know what you mean! I am merely trying to rest and here you are, a pesty woody-bottle thing, disturbing me'.

'*Wood-beetle*,' corrected the wood-beetle. 'Which means that I eat dead wood. This tree, beg your pardon, your *home* is dead wood,' he said. 'I was only going to take a few bites anyway. You wouldn't have even noticed.'

He started to leave, but paused, turned and said, 'I am well aware that everyone thinks I'm a pest, but without *'pests'* like me eating these old, dead trees, there would be no room for new ones now, would there?' The wood-beetle began to scuttle away, 'I shall leave you in peace now. Goodbye!'

Mr Squidgely immediately regretted his remarks. 'Erm, please wait a moment!' he called out. 'I'm sorry for calling you 'pesty'. It's just, well, I *am* stuck and rather tetchy I'm afraid!'

The wood-beetle returned. 'I *knew* you were stuck,' he said. 'Why didn't you just say so?'

Mr Squidgely sighed. 'I was too embarrassed,' he began. 'You see, I stayed inside all winter with a huge pile of acorns; the like of which you've never seen by the way! Now they are all gone and I'm just too big to get out!'

'Ah, the downside of a good harvest!' said the wood-beetle. 'Everyone puts on a little more weight. Nothing that a bit of exercise won't put right, once we get you out of there.'

'And how exactly are we supposed to do that?' asked Mr Squidgely.

The wood-beetle smiled. 'Have you forgotten already? I'm not called a wood-beetle for nothing. I eat wood remember?' He weighed up the situation, rubbing his chin thoughtfully. 'I think I can nibble away around the edges of the hole,' he said. 'But it's quite hard and it might take a long time by myself even though I am quite hungry.' He thought for a moment, and said, 'I need some help with this.' Then he turned again. 'I shan't be long. Don't go away!'

Realising what he had said, the wood-beetle made a sort of apologetic face and scurried off down the tree.

Mr Squidgely waited for what seemed ages before he heard quiet scuttling noises coming from beneath him.

The wood-beetle appeared again, but not alone this time, for even with his limited range of vision, Mr Squidgely could make out dozens of the little creatures.

With a wink to Mr Squidgely and a nod to the others, the wood-beetle and his friends began munching away the hard edges of the entrance to his den, now and again tickling his face and paws with their hairy insect legs.

As the hours passed, Mr Squidgely felt himself being freed up after so long stuck in the hole. Bit by bit, bite by bite, the hole got bigger and bigger until at last, and with great relief, he was able to push with his back legs and pull with his front paws and haul himself out of his den.

Mr Squidgely was so grateful to the wood-beetle and his friends that he allowed them to share his tree. It would be a very long time indeed before they devoured enough of the tree that he would have to find himself a new home, but in the meantime he made sure to get plenty of exercise, especially during the winter feasting season.

— 14 —

THE BEAST OF BUNNY WOOD

*H*ave you ever walked in a wood, perhaps early in the morning or at dusk, and caught a glimpse, a shape or a movement from the corner of your eye of something that your instinct tells you shouldn't be there? Something, a creature maybe, that doesn't quite belong?

There are tales abound of strange things lurking in woods everywhere, and Bunny Wood is no exception.

Here the woodland creatures, fairies and even bogles sometimes talk in hushed voices of a being known simply as 'The Beast of Bunny Wood' which, so the legend goes, is able to turn creatures to stone.

Needless to say, each year mothers tell stories about the Beast to their children, warning them about the dangers of straying too far from their dens, especially in spring when new-borns are at their most vulnerable.

The thing is, when you are small it is very easy to lose your way among the bramble bushes and bindweed, especially when you can't look over the top; and that is exactly what happened one day to a pair of bunny siblings, Barnaby and Beatrix, who were playing hide and seek. So involved were they in their game that they didn't notice just how far they were straying from the safety of their warren, and suddenly they realised that they were indeed lost.

The two young bunnies had found themselves in an area of tangled undergrowth and old logs, covered with moss and ivy, none of which they recognised.

The more they tried to find their way out of what seemed a jungle to such small creatures, the deeper they went into the dark, twisted mass.

How long they had been lost, they had no idea, but they felt sure that it was getting late and that their mother would be very worried about them soon. Perhaps if they stayed were they were, she would come looking for them and they would all go home, have supper, and everything would be fine.

Just then there was a noise, a kind of throaty rumbling sound they had never heard before, and it was close by, very close indeed.

 The two small bunnies held each other tightly, looking around nervously.

'What was that?' whispered Beatrix

'I don't know,' said Barnaby, his hushed voice trembling. 'I think we should move.'

'But which way?'

'Let's keep going forward. Whatever it is, it's right behind us.'

Clinging on to each other, the two little bunnies went deeper and deeper into the undergrowth, jumping at the slightest rustling sound, until they came to a small clearing and froze, eyes wide open, at what they saw before them.

Partly buried in the tangled ivy and dead moss-covered wood was a rabbit. A large rabbit, bigger than their father; but that wasn't what stopped them in their tracks. What they were looking at was a rabbit completely motionless and made of stone.

The two bunnies looked at one another, then back at the stone rabbit and clung to each other even tighter. So it was true! The story of the 'Beast of Bunny Wood' that turned woodland creatures to stone wasn't just a story after all. What's more, they were sure that they had disturbed the Beast.

'What are we going to do?' asked Beatrix tearfully. 'I don't want to end up like this poor rabbit here!'

'Shush now,' whispered Barnaby, trying to be brave. 'We have to be quiet and hide until we can find a way to get back home.'

They heard a rustling from behind them, along with the same throaty, rumbling sound.

'Come on,' said Barnaby. 'We'll hide behind the stone rabbit.' He took hold of his sister's paw and pulled her over to the statue-like rabbit, where they quickly ducked down and flattened their ears. Not a moment too soon as it turned out, for at that very moment the Beast entered the clearing. Even though they couldn't see it, the two bunnies knew instinctively that it was indeed the Beast. That terrible rumbling sound was very close now, and the bunnies could sense its presence.

Barnaby and Beatrix kept as still and as quiet as they possibly could, even though both were trembling with fear; but it wasn't enough. The Beast had keen senses too, and it discovered their hiding place in an instant.

The two bunnies looked up and, with nowhere else to go, found themselves staring into two fearsome yellow eyes which, in turn, were staring back at them beneath a rather stern frown.

Then a deep voice from a mouth they could not yet see said, 'Who are you? What are you doing in my patch?'

'It's him!' cried Beatrix, terrified. 'It's the Beast, and he's going to turn us to stone!'

Barnaby stood up, bravely positioning himself in front of his sister to protect her.

The yellow-eyed Beast lifted its head to show its whole face over the stone rabbit. The rest of its face looked as fearsome as the eyes; pale gingery-coloured thick fur and downturned mouth fringed with long, thick whiskers.

 'What's that?' said the Beast. '*Who's* going to turn you to stone?'

Barnaby swallowed and spoke up, trying to sound as big and grown up as he could. 'You're the Beast our mother told us about, aren't you? The Beast that turns creatures to stone, like this rabbit here.'

The Beast stared back at Barnaby for a moment, then its mouth turned into a smile, and its fearsome yellow eyes softened a little. 'Ha!' it said, laughing and showing its sharp teeth. '*That* old rabbits' tale! The 'Beast of Bunny Wood' is it?' Then it leaned down to face Barnaby, their noses almost touching. 'What if I was to tell you there's no such thing?' it said.

Barnaby looked the Beast in the eye, trying to appear brave, even though he was trembling. 'If there is no such thing,' he said, 'then who are you, and what turned this poor rabbit to stone?'

The Beast lifted a paw, resting it on top of the stone rabbit, drumming away with exposed sharp claws. Barnaby instinctively took a step back and pulled his frightened sister closer.

'Allow me to introduce myself,' said the Beast. 'I am *not* a beast. I am Old Ginger; on account of the fact that I'm an old ginger cat!' He waved the other paw in the air. 'This happens to be my patch,' he said.

'Then why were you chasing us?' said Barnaby, 'and what about this poor rabbit here?'

The ginger cat laughed again. 'I wasn't chasing you. You woke me up with your playing around. Then I got to thinking that two little bunnies like yourselves oughtn't to be here, and perhaps they might be lost.' He smiled a more welcoming smile. 'I was merely trying to help you, that's all.'

Barnaby, however, was still a little wary. 'Then how did this poor rabbit get turned to stone?'

Old Ginger tapped his claws on the stone rabbit. 'This was never a real rabbit my dear little fellow,' he said. 'This is what bogles call an "ornament."

'A ormanent?' said Barnaby.

'An *or-na-ment*,' said the cat. 'You see, bogles sometimes like to have ornaments of woodland creatures around their house. They are not real creatures, just creatures *made* from stone. This here rabbit is an ornament that was owned by a bogle who lived nearby a long time ago. Then, he grew tired of it and threw it away; and here it's been ever since.'

By now, both Barnaby and Beatrix were facing the cat, less afraid, and listening intently.

'But how do you know all this?' asked Barnaby.

Old Ginger sighed, and looked wistfully into the distance. 'How do I know? Well, I know because I once lived in the same house as that bogle and this ornament.' He looked at them both, a little sadness in his eyes. 'You see, bogles can grow tired of anything, not just ornaments. I was once a bogle's cat; happy enough, I suppose. Then one day, he made up his mind to move somewhere else – I don't know where – and he threw out anything he didn't want to take with him.'

Beatrix spoke up, no longer afraid, but feeling sorrowful for the cat. 'You mean the bogle threw you out too?'

'Yes, little one,' said Old Ginger. 'So now you can see how this story of the Beast has come about.'

Barnaby nodded. It all made perfect sense. A whole scary story made up out of quite ordinary things.

'Anyway,' said Old Ginger. 'I think I should be showing you the way back home. I'll bet your mother will be wondering where you've got to.'

'Oh, yes please!' cried Beatrix, not the slightest bit afraid of the old cat now.

'Come on then,' said Old Ginger. 'Follow me.'

Within no time at all, Old Ginger had guided the two little bunnies through the undergrowth and back to their own patch, just in time for supper.

'Why don't you come and have supper with us?' Barnaby asked. 'I'm sure mother wouldn't mind and we could tell her all about how the 'Beast' is not really real after all.'

Old Ginger smiled. 'I'll tell you what,' he said. 'Why don't we just keep it our secret? Sometimes a scary story is not a bad thing if it stops little ones like you wandering too far from home and getting themselves lost, is it? And besides, it might just help to keep the bogles away too, don't you think?'

'Good idea,' said Barnaby. 'But will you be alright on your own?'

Old Ginger twirled his whiskers between sharp claws. 'Oh, I've managed perfectly well so far,' he said. 'We cats... er... 'beasts' know how to take care of ourselves, you know.' With a wink and a flick of his stripy ginger tail, he turned and disappeared into the undergrowth.

I have it on good authority that Barnaby and Beatrix never told anyone else about their encounter with Old Ginger and that, to this day, the legend of 'The Beast of Bunny Wood' lives on.

—— 15 ——

THE VAIN FAIRY

$\mathcal{T}$here once was a fairy, a pretty little thing, but also quite vain it has to be said.

Rather than play with the other fairies and woodland creatures, this particular fairy would spend most of her day sitting by the pond, admiring her reflection in the water.

The thought of getting dirty from playing in muddy puddles, or allowing her hair to be seen uncombed and straggly, quite frankly appalled her.

Instead she would collect flowers and feathers to make adornments for her hair, reddening her lips and blushing her cheeks with rowanberry juice. Then she would spend hours adjusting this and altering that, until she was satisfied with the result.

One sunny spring morning, the fairy was admiring herself as usual in the mirrored surface of the pond.

'Oh my, how beautiful I look today,' she thought. 'How perfectly lovely! Why, I surely must be the loveliest creature in all of Bunny Wood!'

Just as she was marvelling at the wonderful rich colour of her berry juice lipstick, the water began to ripple, distorting her features and interrupting her self-adoration.

Annoyed, the fairy looked up to see what had 'broken' her mirror. What she saw was quite the most beautiful thing she had ever set eyes on. Swimming towards her, snowy white feathers shining like a halo in the morning sun, was a swan.

'But wait,' thought the fairy. 'How can this possibly be? Surely *I* am the most beautiful creature in all of Bunny Wood, and yet...'

The swan paddled up to the fairy. 'Good morning,' she said, cheerfully. 'What a lovely morning it is.'

The fairy was almost lost for words. 'Yes... er... good morning to you.' But she was unable to take her eyes off the loveliness before her. 'She has no make-up,' she thought. 'No colouring at all in her feathers. Why then does she look so perfectly lovely?'

'Come closer,' said the fairy. 'So I can get a good look at you.'

The swan swam to the edge of the pond and the fairy looked her up and down. 'What is it that makes you so very beautiful?' she asked.

The swan smiled, a little embarrassed. 'Oh, I don't know about that my dear,' she said. 'I'm just happy with what Mother Nature gave me. If that makes me beautiful, then it's all down to her.' With that, the swan said goodbye and set off in search of more pond weed for breakfast.

The fairy sat down on a toadstool, somewhat vexed. After some serious thinking and head-scratching, she decided that, in order to truly become the most beautiful creature in all of Bunny Wood, she should wash off every trace of make-up and scrub her skin all over until it was pure white like a swan. So she flew over to an old hollowed out tree stump that was filled with rain water, removed all her floral adornments, climbed in and began to scrub herself with a clump of damp moss.

Just as the fairy had removed the last of the berry juice from her face, a damselfly happened by, alighting daintily on the edge of the tree stump.

'Good morning,' said the damselfly. 'Isn't it a lovely day?'

The fairy looked at the damselfly, dressed in radiant cobalt blue and thought it was the most beautiful colour she had ever seen.

'Where did you get such a lovely colour from?' asked the fairy. 'You look so very beautiful.'

'You are very kind,' said the damselfly. 'I don't know about beautiful. I am what Mother Nature made me, and it was she who gave me this colour.'

The damselfly looked at the fairy. 'I hope you don't mind me saying,' he began, 'but you look a little pale. Are you feeling unwell?'

The fairy looked down at herself. It was true. Alongside the beautiful damselfly her skin looked pale and washed out, not at all like the pure white feathers of the swan.

'I hope you feel better soon,' said the damselfly, and flew off.

The fairy climbed out of her bath and sat on the ground, head in hands, thinking hard. 'If I can't be like a beautiful swan, then I shall be like a radiant damselfly. I shall find a lovely blue and cover myself in it. Then everyone will see that I am the most beautiful creature in all of Bunny Wood!'

Her mind made up, the fairy flew off in search of a lovely blue. In a small meadow close to Bunny Wood she came across a patch of grape hyacinths, their perfect little blue flowers clustered like bunches of grapes. 'Such a lovely blue,' she thought. 'These will be perfect!' Then she proceeded to pick the flowers and rub them all over her face and body until she was blue from top to bottom.

Nearby, a Burnet moth feeding on a clump of ragwort flowers caught sight of the fairy and flew over to say hello. 'Are you cold?' asked the moth.

'No, I'm not cold,' said the fairy. 'Why do you ask?'

The moth looked her up and down. 'I couldn't help noticing how blue you look,' it said. 'I thought you might be feeling a little chilly.'

The fairy was disappointed, because she had been expecting a compliment on her lovely blueness. Then she noticed the moth's wings; such a lovely dark grey with rich ruby red spots. Her own wings were quite pale and transparent, so as to be barely visible. Now, if she had wings like the Burnet moth, how could she fail to be the most beautiful creature in all of Bunny Wood?

'Your wings are so beautiful,' said the fairy. 'Where did you get them?'

'Why, thank you,' said the moth. 'I didn't get them from anywhere. They were given to me by Mother Nature when I changed from a caterpillar. I never really thought of them as beautiful. As long as they carry me from flower to flower, that's all that really matters, isn't it?'

The moth turned to leave. 'Anyway, I must dash. There's a lot of ragwort to get through today. I hope you warm up soon and get your colour back!'

Feeling somewhat frustrated, the fairy decided to wash off the now dull, fading blue and find something with which to paint her wings like those of the Burnet moth; so she began scouring Bunny Wood for the materials she needed.

The first thing the fairy found was a tree stump that had been struck by lightning in last summer's storms. The dark grey ash was exactly the right colour for her Burnet wings, so she mixed some with a little water in an acorn cap. Then she remembered the rowanberry juice she had used for her lips and cheeks. That would be perfect for the ruby red spots.

So, after her second bath of the day, the fairy set about painting her wings, using small white feathers, the kind that can be found all over Bunny Wood, as paintbrushes.

After a goodly length of time, for it was quite difficult twisting and turning and painting and dabbing, the fairy's newly-painted wings were finished. Looking over her shoulders, she was satisfied that they looked exactly the same as those of the lovely Burnet moth.

As she was admiring her colourful artwork a chirpy little voice said, 'My goodness, what lovely wings! Where did you get them?'

The fairy turned to see a blackbird sitting on a low branch. 'At last!' she thought. 'A compliment!'

'Why, thank you,' said the fairy. 'Mother Nature gave them to me,' she lied, not wanting to appear false in any way.

'Well,' said the blackbird, 'Mother Nature certainly did you proud. They are the most beautiful wings I've ever seen!'

The fairy almost, but not quite, blushed at the compliment, for it was the very least she had hoped to hear.

'You simply must come and show all my friends,' said the blackbird. 'They will all be green with envy!'

This was exactly what the fairy wanted to hear. 'Of course,' she said. 'I'm more than happy to show them off. Lead the way!'

The blackbird flew down and pointed across the pond. 'Follow me,' she said. 'It's not far.'

The blackbird took off towards the other side of the pond and the fairy flapped her new Burnet wings and set off to follow her, but just moments into the flight she felt something was wrong.

You see, what had happened was that there was so much weight and clagginess from the ash and berry paint, the fairy's wings just didn't work properly, and she felt herself falling like a stone.

Fortunately, if you could call it fortune, the fairy landed not with a thump on the hard ground, but with a squelch into the mud at the edge of the pond.

Finally, exasperated and exhausted from her attempts to become the most beautiful creature in all of Bunny Wood, the fairy sat in the mud, folded her arms and let out a deep sigh.

In annoyance and frustration, the fairy began to slap the mud either side of her, slapping so hard that mud was flying everywhere, covering her hands, her legs and her face.

Then the strangest thing happened. The fairy started to laugh; a sort of loopy laugh to begin with, but then she realised that she was actually enjoying herself. In fact, the more she slapped and the muddier she became, the more she laughed.

The fairy was by now causing quite a commotion, so much so that birds, bunnies, squirrels and all manner of creatures came to see what all the fuss was about. What they saw was a fairy, covered in mud, but as happy a soul as any could be.

The swan, who had been pulling up pond weed nearby, swam over to see what was going on.

'Why are you laughing so?' asked the swan.

'I'm having fun!' said the fairy. 'And, for the first time, I don't even care what I look like. Have I gone mad do you think?'

The swan smiled down at the muddy fairy and shook her head. 'No, my dear,' she said. 'You haven't gone mad. What a pleasure it is to see such a lovely, happy, dirty face. Why, I declare that you must surely be the most beautiful creature in all of Bunny Wood!'

—— 16 ——

MOONFLOWER

*A*night fairy is a very different kettle of fish altogether than the fairies you might be more familiar with from stories or, if you are one of the lucky few, might have glimpsed on a warm spring day whilst walking in a secluded wood.

Unlike those happy-go-lucky souls who love to play in the sunshine with other woodland creatures, perhaps occasionally playing tricks on them, night fairies have a much darker nature, as befits their nocturnal habitat.

Fairies, as you know, can sometimes be either good or downright mischievous, as their fancy takes them. But night fairies are *never* good. They can, if the mood takes them, be evil, vindictive creatures, not to be trifled with and ready to take your soul if you have the misfortune to encounter one on a moonlit night deep in the woods.

Once upon a long time ago a fairy was born at midnight, under a full moon. The timing of this event was to set the course of her life. Destiny had declared that she was to be a night fairy.

Her mother gave her the name of Moonflower and did her best to raise her in the ways of her own kind. But, try as she might, she could not keep her daughter awake during daylight hours to play with the other fairies or other woodland creatures. As soon as she was able to, much to her mother's increasing anxiety, Moonflower would leave her home under the twisted roots of an old beech tree at dusk; returning just before dawn to sleep the whole day.

Moonflower was, of course, aware from an early age that she was quite different from other fairies. Aside from being wingless, true to her name, she bloomed at night, her eyes, as black as coal, able to see everything; even under the darkest, moonless sky.

She feasted on mushrooms which grew in the dark and damp places, learning from some mysterious age–old instinct which of the fungi would enhance her night fairy attributes.

Then the day arrived when Moonflower had blossomed into a fully fledged fairy. It was time for her to leave home. There was a tear in her mother's eye when she bade her daughter farewell, pleading with her to try and be nice to those she encountered.

Moonflower looked at her, a furrowed brow shading her dark eyes, and said simply, 'Goodnight mother.' Then she left; disappearing into the night without as much as a backward glance.

The first thing that Moonflower needed to do was to find herself a home. On her previous nocturnal outings, she had seen a pair of bats roosting in a hole high up in an elm tree. Naturally, being a night fairy, her instincts told her not to waste precious energy looking for something when she already knew where said 'something' was to be had.

Despite not having been born with the delicate butterfly or feathered wings of daytime fairies, Moonflower knew that there was another way for her to take to the air.

Scouring the area around the roots of the tree, she soon found what she was looking for. A clump of ragwort grew nearby and she set about breaking off a sturdy stem. As she cleaned the stem of flowers and leaves, she remembered to make an apology to the fairy gods for disturbing the enchanted plant, as her instincts told her, and then sat astride the stem.

With a little willpower, Moonflower was able to rise up into the air on the ragwort stem, fly up to the bats' roost and, with nothing more than a threatening stare from her dark eyes, evict the occupants.

Happy, or as happy as a perpetually frowning creature could be, in her new home, Moonflower's next task was to collect some ingredients with which to create a night fairy's 'special' concoctions.

No-one had taught Moonflower about how to go about preparing these concoctions; she simply knew what to gather; deadly nightshade berries, bindweed flowers, from which her name 'Moonflower' came, ivy leaves, crab apples and various fungi which would be poisonous to you and I. All of these she stored in the hole in readiness to prepare what some might call 'magical' potions, but which to her were simply essentials for her particular way of life.

She then fashioned a wand of sorts out of a twig from a wild apple tree, which grew on the bank overlooking Bunny Wood Lake.

Perched on the lip of her new roost and swooshing the night air with her wand, Moonflower looked out over her dark domain, now fully prepared to unleash some seriously wicked mischief.

That age-old instinct that Moonflower was born with again told her that capturing the souls of other creatures, especially those who were not particularly nice, would make her stronger and, naturally, she knew just the right potion to help her.

She set about crushing up some ivy leaves, adding a bit of this and that from her store of ingredients. When she had finished, Moonflower carefully put the mixture into an acorn cap, adding a little water to make it drinkable, and then sealed the cap with tree resin. Now all she had to do was find a victim.

Night time was the time when particularly nasty bogles prowled the wood and lake, catching frogs, fish, ducks or any other creature they could lay their hands on. Moonflower had seen several of these bogles on her earlier nocturnal wanderings, and knew exactly where to find them.

Holding the potion carefully in one hand and grasping the ragwort stem firmly with the other, Moonflower launched herself from the roost and flew across the lake to Pigeon Wood. Here she settled down, hiding in a cluster of ink cap mushrooms and waited.

Patience was not one of Moonflower's virtues, if indeed she had any virtues to begin with. Nonetheless, she summoned all her considerable willpower to remain as still and quiet as she could.

Fortunately, she didn't have to wait too long before she heard a rustling in the undergrowth.

Her sensitive eyes easily picked up the outline of a bogle, and he was heading in her direction.

Now bogles have poor vision in the dark, so Moonflower had no concerns that he would see her hiding among the mushrooms.

As the bogle drew closer, she could see he was carrying a large sack; large enough for a brace of ducks, she imagined.

 Moonflower felt no particular care or protective instincts for the creatures that lived around Bunny Wood Lake; her only interest was in stealing the bogle's soul. She watched as he began creeping around the water's edge, searching for sleeping ducks.

When the bogle found what he was looking for, there was an almighty commotion as he launched himself into the sleeping ducks; the sound of quacking and flapping filled the night air.

When the brief kerfuffle died down, Moonflower watched as the bogle stood up, an agitated duck in each hand, and danced a little victory jig before depositing the hapless creatures into his sack.

This was the moment that Moonflower had been waiting for.

As the bogle was tying up the sack, she stepped out from behind the mushrooms and approached him, wearing a forlorn expression.

'Can you help me please?' said Moonflower as she drew close to the bogle.

He looked down in surprise, as he certainly didn't expect to see anyone else around at this time of night.

Moonflower spoke again. 'Please, kind sir, can you help me?'

'Help you?' thought the bogle. 'I'd sooner 'ave you for supper, along with these 'ere ducks.' But he couldn't help but be a little curious as to what this strange-looking creature wanted, so he feigned a smile and said, 'Help you, little one? Of course I will. What is it you'll be wanting?'

Moonflower held out the potion-filled acorn cap. 'I have this potion,' she began, 'which helps me to fly. And as you can see I don't have wings like other fairies do.' She turned around to show the bogle that, indeed, she had no wings.

The bogle was a little puzzled, but nonetheless intrigued. 'So what will you be wanting my help for?'

Moonflower continued. 'You see, the seal has dried too hard and I can't get into it to drink the potion.'

An idea began to form in the bogle's somewhat limited imagination. The idea of a potion that could make him fly would surely enable him to catch even more ducks.

'Why, of course I'll 'elp you my dear,' he said, putting on his best 'gentlemanly' voice. 'Come over 'ere and I'll break that seal in two shakes.'

Moonflower held up the acorn cap and the bogle dropped the sack, bent down and took the potion.

He broke the seal in no time at all. Then, with a snigger, he lifted the cup to his lips. 'You is goin' to need some 'elp after I drinks this,' he said. 'I likes a bit of fairy cake after a tasty duck fuddle!' Then he downed the potion, licked his lips and grinned a yellow-toothed grin.

'Now it's your turn for the sack!' he said, bending down to make a grab for Moonflower, who just stared at him with her cold, dark eyes.

But, as he leaned forward, the bogle's eyes crossed and his legs wobbled. 'Ooh,' he slurred, 'I've come over all...'

He never finished the sentence. Instead he wobbled some more, swayed a little from side to side, and finally toppled backwards, crashing onto the ground with a dull thud.

Moonflower was delighted; you could tell this by the way she raised one eyebrow and the corners of her mouth turned up ever so slightly.

She bent over the bogle's face and checked his eyes, which were now turned up in their sockets. Then she circled his head three times with her wand, put her mouth to his, grimacing at the rancid smell, and extracted his soul in one deep draw of her breath.

Moonflower felt a surge of energy through her body and the bogle was, alas, no more.

As she turned to leave, she heard the ducks flapping and quacking in the bogle's sack. 'Oh, do be quiet!' she said. 'The bogle's dead, so think yourselves lucky!'

The noise continued. Moonflower was on the point of grabbing her ragwort stem to fly off when something, some faint glimmer of goodness perhaps, made her stop and untie the sack, releasing the captured ducks.

'Oh, thank you! Thank you!' said the ducks. 'You saved our lives. How can we ever repay you?'

Moonflower glared at the ducks. 'You can thank me by shooing away and keeping quiet. Don't you dare tell anyone that I let you go, or I'll come back and take *your* souls too!'

You see, in her mind, Moonflower had a reputation to keep. If word got around that she was in any way soft-hearted, no creature or bogle would be scared of her and give her the respect she deserved as a night fairy.

Of course, Moonflower had no interest in the innocent souls of woodland creatures, but better they thought that she did.

And so began the rather uneasy relationship between the night fairy and the creatures of Bunny Wood Lake. Moonflower continued to develop her powers, stealing the souls of bogles who dared to venture out for a spot of night time hunting or fishing, while the woodland creatures, thankful of a degree of protection, kept their distance whenever she was doing her nightly rounds.

So beware! If ever you decide to make mischief in the woodland after dark, more than likely there will be someone watching; and it just might be *your* soul that the night fairy is after next.

—— 17 ——

THE MOUSE WHO WOULD BE KING

*U*nbeknown to most folk, there is a secluded, dark corner of Bunny Wood, where it is so dark and dank that even bluebells refuse to grow there, wherein lay an abandoned mushroom village. No-one knew exactly how the village came to be abandoned, but rumour had it that an evil bogle happened by one day and scared all the villagers away.

Now there was a mouse, a traveller by nature, whose head was full of fanciful notions, who happened to be strolling through the wood on a particularly sunny day; carefree and whistling merry tunes as he went on his way, as was his habit on days like this.

Quite by accident, the mouse stumbled into the mushroom village. 'Hello!' he called out, for he did not know that the village was deserted, 'Hello!' he called again. 'I am but a poor travelling mouse, and I should like very much to rest awhile in your beautiful village.' But the only reply to his calling out was silence.

The mouse went from mushroom to mushroom, peeking inside and calling out until he had checked each and every one, but they were all empty.

'Mmm,' he thought. 'If no-one lives here, then I can have my pick of them to stay in.'

The mouse looked around, and found the biggest mushroom hut of them all. 'I shall have this one,' he said to himself. 'This one is the grand palace of all mushroom huts. Fit for a king it is!'

Then he had an idea. 'Yes!' he cried. 'Fit for a king! I shall be king of the whole village!'

'What I need now,' he thought, 'is a crown. I shall make me a crown!'

The mouse scampered around the village, collecting bits of twig and moss. Then he sat down in front of the big hut and set about weaving the twigs and moss into a passable semblance of a crown, adding a few rowan berries here and there for jewels, and placed it on his head. Then he stood up, held his head high and made a royal declaration of sorts.

'Hear me everyone!' he boomed, as much as a mouse's voice *can* boom, 'I am King of this here village; henceforth to be known as Ambrosia, on account of my name being Ambrose! All hail and bow down to King Ambrose!' but, of course, there was no-one to hear him, let alone bow down to him.

Now that Ambrose had declared himself to be King, he felt rather tired. Finding a nice bit of soft, green moss in a hollow near to his new mushroom palace, he carefully removed his crown, setting it down next to him, laid on his luxurious green bed and fell into a right royal sleep.

In his sleep, Ambrose dreamt he heard someone sobbing. The noise woke him, as often happens in dreams, but the thing was, when he woke up he could *actually* hear someone sobbing.

Forcing open his sleepy eyes, he looked around and there, seated on a large spotted toadstool was a pale figure, a fairy with delicate butterfly wings, sobbing away.

Ambrose stood up and approached the fairy. 'Who are you?' he asked in his best kingly voice.

The fairy looked up at him, her eyes dark from all the crying. 'My name is Lily,' she said in between sobs. 'Who are you?'

'I am King Ambrose,' said the mouse. 'And this here is my Kingdom, the Kingdom of Ambrosia.'

'Oh,' said the fairy. 'I didn't know this was a Kingdom. Pardon my intrusion, your Highness.'

'Well that's alright,' said Ambrose. 'I've not been King for long. But tell me, why are you crying so?'

'Haven't you heard?' asked Lily.

'Heard what exactly?'

'About the terrible bogle who's clearing out the wood?'

'No,' said Ambrose, 'I've just arrived.' He looked around. 'Is that why there's no-one in the village?'

'Yes,' Lily replied. 'There were lots of creatures living here, but the bogle frightened them all away.' She began to sob again. 'He wants to get rid of everyone and cut down all the trees to build himself a house.'

'A bogle house? Here? As King of Ambrosia I cannot allow that. In fact, I absolutely forbid it!'

'But what can you do?' asked Lily.

'I will challenge him to a duel!' said Ambrose.

Lily smiled at Ambrose. 'Oh my,' she said. 'What a brave and noble king you are.' Then her face saddened a little. 'But I fear the bogle is too big and strong even for you.'

Ambrose stroked his little mousey chin thoughtfully. 'Mmm,' he said. 'Bogles *are* quite big... but, then again, they are also quite stupid creatures.'

'That is true,' said Lily. 'But even so, how can we stop him?'

'We need to think of something, 'said Ambrose. 'And soon!'

So Ambrose paced regally around the village, wishing he had made a thinking cap instead of a crown, while Lily sat quietly on the toadstool deep in thought.

After a short while, Lily jumped up excitedly; her wings fluttering so fast that she almost hit her head on an overhanging tree branch.

'I think I've got an idea!' she said.

'Tell me! Tell me!' said Ambrose. 'Are we going to kill him?'

Lily settled back onto the toadstool and beckoned Ambrose to come closer.

'Surely you know that, by woodland law, we can't just kill someone; no matter how evil they may be?'

Ambrose adopted a proud, regal pose, frowning at the little fairy in puzzlement.

'What kind of silly law is that?' he said. 'As King of Ambrosia, I can make any law I wish, and I say let's kill him!'

Lily put her hand on Ambrose's shoulder.

'Woodland law is what makes us strong,' she said. 'It binds us to each other and to Mother Nature. It's the only way we can truly live in peace and harmony together.'

'I see,' said Ambrose. 'Remind me to have you write my kingly speeches. So, what's the plan?'

'Well,' Lily began. 'Woodland law also decrees that challenges can be set to solve disputes, and that whoever wins the challenge wins the dispute. So we challenge the bogle and, if he loses, he will have to leave.'

'And if he wins?'

'You said it yourself,' said Lily. 'Bogles are quite stupid creatures.'

'Mmm,' thought Ambrose. 'I really hope I'm right.' Then, out loud. 'What if he won't leave after he loses?'

'He has to,' said Lily. 'Woodland law applies to all, even bogles. If he refuses to leave, Mother Nature will punish him severely.'

'So, what's the challenge to be?'

Lily looked around to make sure that no-one was around to hear, which of course there wasn't.

'I remember a time,' she began, 'when my grandmother told me of a dispute challenge. I can't remember what the dispute was, but I do remember the challenge.'

Ambrose was listening intently.

Lily continued. 'There were three riddles asked, each one harder than the other. The challenge was to answer all three correctly. To this day I can still remember those riddles.'

Ambrose pondered for a moment, then asked, 'Who won the challenge?'

'That I don't know,' Lily replied. 'But they are hard riddles indeed and, if the bogle is as stupid as we think he is, then he will surely lose.'

'I don't know,' said Ambrose. 'It all sounds a bit risky to me. Let's just kill him instead.'

Lily shook her head. 'No. Mother Nature would punish us most severely. We have to do this properly or not at all.'

Reluctantly, Ambrose agreed.

'So we simply need to find the bogle and challenge him then?'

'I'm sure if he knows we're here, he'll find *us.*' said Lily. 'Then we put our faith in the woodland law.'

They decided that the best way to attract the bogle's attention would be to start a fire, just a small one, so that if he happened to be anywhere near Bunny Wood he would see the smoke and come to investigate.

So they set about collecting dry twigs and leaves, which are especially good for making smoke, and piled them up in a clearing away from trees and bushes.

Ambrose looked on in awe as the fairy created sparks to light the fire by rubbing a couple of stones together.

Once the twigs and leaves were alight, thick smoke began to rise up through the trees in no time at all.

'What do we do now?' asked Ambrose.

'Now we wait,' said Lily. 'When the bogle arrives, you, as King of Ambrosia, will challenge him and I will do the rest.'

As they waited, they stoked the fire with more leaves, creating even more smoke that could clearly be seen well beyond the borders of Bunny Wood.

Well, they didn't have to wait too long before the sound of cracking twigs and rustling leaves could be heard; someone or something heavy-footed was fast approaching the mushroom village.

Ambrose and Lily stood side by side, defiantly awaiting the arrival of what they surely knew to be the loathsome bogle.

Sure enough, with a final crashing of brambles and twigs, a fearsome-looking figure appeared, towering above the pair.

'Who started this fire in my wood?' roared the bogle. He looked down at Ambrose and Lily with angry red eyes. 'Was it you? I'll 'ave you for trespassin' so I will. Then I'll roast you on this 'ere fire and eat you for supper!'

Lily nudged Ambrose with her elbow. 'Now,' she whispered.

Ambrose stepped forward, adjusted his crown and spoke to the bogle, projecting his voice as much as he could, so as to make himself sound important.

'*Your* wood?' he said. 'Well excuse me, but I happen to be the king here and this village and this wood are under *my* rule!'

The bogle paused, gave a puzzled frown then began to laugh; a horrible cackling sound that made Ambrose wince.

When he had regained his composure, the bogle bent down and addressed the pair of them.

'If you two don't scarper this instant you is goin' to be very 'ot... very soon. Now be off!'

Ambrose could smell the bogle's rancid breath, so close was he, but stood his ground.

'By virtue of the woodland law, I challenge you for the right to live in this wood,' he said.

The bogle stood up, a little surprised.

'Ooh, woodland law is it? A challenge eh? So you want to fight me do you, you little pipsqueak?' He threw his head back, guffawing loudly.

Just then, Lily stepped forward.

'I do believe,' she said, 'that, by woodland law, it is up to the challenger to set the terms of the challenge.' She glanced at Ambrose and nodded.

'Yes,' said Ambrose. 'My, erm... *assistant* is quite correct. And if you refuse my challenge then it is *you* who must leave, never to return.'

The bogle, believing himself to be far superior and much more intelligent than a scrawny little mouse – bogles tend to have a rather high opinion of themselves – scratched his straggly beard and nodded.

'Never let it be said that I doesn't respect the woodland law. I accepts your stupid challenge,' he said. 'But be warned, when I wins it, you two is goin' to be roasted into a fuddle!'

Ambrose looked nervously at Lily and whispered, 'I hope you're right about this or we're done for.'

Lily took a deep breath and stepped forward.

'As the king's *assistant,* it falls on me to present the challenge on his behalf,' she said. 'And it is this. I will ask of you three riddles. Answer all three correctly and the wood shall be yours. But, if you fail to answer all three, then you must leave, never to return. Do you accept?'

The bogle, full of confidence, waved his warty hand. 'Ask away,' he said. 'My brains is bigger than a 'undred of you!'

'Very well,' said Lily. 'Here is the first riddle. What always runs but never walks, often murmurs, never talks, has a bed but never sleeps, has a mouth but never eats?'

Ambrose looked at Lily, eyes wide open. 'That's a hard one,' he whispered. 'He'll never know the answer to that!'

The bogle frowned, pondered, scratched his beard and pondered some more. Then a smug smile appeared on his face.

'I knows this one,' he said. 'It's a river, ain't it?'

Ambrose gasped, disappointedly and Lily nodded silently.

'Yes! Yes!' cried the bogle.' Give me another!'

Lily again took a deep breath and asked, 'You saw me where I never was and where I could not be. And yet within that very place, my face you often see. What am I?'

'That's a *really* hard one,' thought Ambrose, studying the bogle's face as he turned the riddle over in his apparently not-quite-so-stupid brain.

The bogle pondered on the riddle for quite some time; frowning, scratching his beard and pacing around.

'Aha!' he cried out at last. 'Thought you 'ad me with this one didn't you? But I think you'll find that the answer is a reflection!'

Ambrose looked at Lily for any sign that the bogle was wrong but, again, she nodded silently. 'One more chance,' he thought. 'Then a bogle roast we shall be!'

The bogle meanwhile was dancing around, shrieking loudly and gleefully. 'Come on! Come on!' he cried out. 'Ask me the last one quickly, for all this brain work is makin' me 'ungry!'

Lily glanced at Ambrose, who was by now looking distinctly worried, and smiled.

She turned to the bogle and said, 'Here is the final riddle. Remember, if you can't answer it you have to leave for good, never to return. Agreed?'

Impatient and full of confidence, the bogle said, 'Yes! Yes! Yes! Agreed! Now just get on with it!'

'In that case,' said Lily. 'Say my name and I disappear. What am I?'

The bogle looked quite puzzled now as he paced around searching for the answer. The more he paced, and the more he puzzled, the more confident Ambrose grew until at last the bogle spoke.

'Argh! You fiendish fairy! I don't know! I don't know! What's the answer? Tell me, or it'll be you wot disappears!'

Ambrose at last breathed a sigh of relief, while Lily stood her ground, squaring up to the bogle.

'The answer is to remain a secret,' she said. 'And now you must keep your word, according to woodland law, and leave us in peace.'

The bogle's face squirmed with anger. 'I will not go!' he cried.' This is *my* wood! You cannot make me leave!'

Ambrose looked at Lily with a *what are we going to do now?* Kind of shrug, but the fairy merely smiled at him and gave a little wink, before addressing the bogle.

'Very well,' she said. 'I will be generous and give you one more chance; one final riddle to decide. Are you ready?'

The bogled smiled a wicked smile, while Ambrose looked at Lily open-mouthed, not quite believing what she was doing.

'Oh yes,' he said. 'One more riddle if you please.'

At that moment, it seemed as if the whole world, not just Bunny Wood, was waiting silently for the outcome.

Lily looked up to the sky, her eyes closed for a moment. Then she gave the bogle an uneasy look with eyes so dark, that he instinctively took a step back.

'Your final riddle,' she said, 'is this.' With carefully measured words, Lily posed the question. 'I touch the Earth, I touch the sky, but if I touch you, you'll surely die. What am I?'
The bogle needed only a few brief moments to come up with an answer.

'Now I have you,' he hissed. 'The answer is *lightning*!'

Ambrose's heart sank. Lily nodded gently and took his arm, pulling him a few steps away from the now fading fire.

The bogle danced about, waving his arms in the air.

'Stupid fairy! Stupid mouse! Now I shall be king, and you shall be my supper!'

The bogle was celebrating his 'victory' so much that he didn't notice the sky above them darkening and storm clouds gathering.

Just then there was a deafening crack of thunder. Lily pulled Ambrose to the ground as a blinding bolt of lightning leapt from a dark cloud and struck the still dancing bogle.

I doubt whether the bogle even knew what had hit him, for in an instant there was nothing but a large pile of smouldering ash where he had been.

The dark clouds sped away, leaving a clear blue sky and almost deafening silence.

Ambrose stared at the pile of ash.

'I thought we weren't going to kill him?' he said.

Lily smiled. 'We didn't,' she said. 'Mother Nature did it. This was her way of keeping the woodland law.'

'That last riddle,' said Ambrose. 'You knew what was going to happen didn't you?'

'That was the part I didn't tell you about,' said Lily. 'My grandmother used it to resolve a dispute a long time ago. I was rather hoping the bogle would leave of his own accord, without having to harm him. Anyway, we won't be bothered by him anymore, will we?'

Needless to say, Lily was right and shortly thereafter, the creatures that once inhabited the mushroom village returned, full of joy.

When they heard what had happened, they had no hesitation in officially declaring Ambrose their king and renaming that part of Bunny Wood Ambrosia in his honour.

Ambrose never asked for, nor was ever told the answer to Lily's third riddle; I imagine she preferred to keep it a secret in case of any future disputes. Nevertheless, Ambrose promoted Lily from the position of 'assistant' to that of his queen, on account of her being so clever in solving disputes and, to my knowledge, King Ambrose and Queen Lily rule over the peaceful kingdom of Ambrosia to this day.

If you, dear reader, ever manage to solve Lily's third riddle, do be sure to let me know, but don't tell anyone else!

AFTERWORD

Now that you have met some of the characters that live in and around Bunny Wood and read their tales, why not go in search of your own local woodland space, lake or pond.

If you are quiet, watchful and, above all patient, you might just see similar stories unfolding; stories about life, relationships, hopes, dreams and the delicate balance that holds everything in nature together.

Remember that places like Bunny Wood are precious. It is up to people like us, the friendly bogles, to help try and keep these habitats safe for all the creatures that live there and be proud to call ourselves Mother Nature's helpers.